MIDNIGHT
of the
SOUL

Nicholas J. Nawroth

A Happyland Press Book.

Dedicated to the twins.

(You know who you are.)

HOUR ONE : THE GRAVEYARD

A flash of lightning.

Then, darkness.

The sky cries soft tears.

The burnt-out husk of a Queen Anne mansion looms high on a hill.

A girl weeps quietly in the shadows by the front veranda.

I become mindful of my approach so as not to startle her.

I start to make out the features of this girl when I'm ripped from my dream into the cold, hard dirt of reality.

I awoke flat on my back. My body ached all over. I couldn't see for a few moments. Cold, damp earth seeped into my clothes. The air had the aroma of dead leaves and freshly turned soil. My heart was beating itself into a panic. I sat bolt upright and a small coin fell from my good eye onto my lap. It was rough silver with markings I couldn't decipher. I expected it to feel cold in my fingers, but it was warm. I could've sworn the eye in the center was glowing. Was it my imagination?

I flipped the coin over to reveal another eye trapped within the three-sided prison of an Egyptian necropolis from antiquity. It stared at me with a piercing intensity. I instinctively reached up and brushed my fingers over my right eye with a minutia of melancholy. I never could see with it. Not ordinary things, that is. My dead eye illuminated a kaleidoscope of colors that guided me, warned me of danger, and saved my life many times over.

Somehow I felt I needed this token, so I secured it in one of the small unoccupied pouches on my belt of useful things. I was still a bit disoriented. Something was bothering me. My dead eye hurt. That was never a good sign.

I looked up to find two enormous trees locked together in an eternal embrace. One was truly beautiful and full of life. It wore its pretty patterned bark like a cloak underneath a vibrant canopy of green leaves. Even the grass growing around its trunk was lush and fertile, and smelled of spring.

But this expression of life couldn't mask the smell of dead leaves that wafted from its partner. Shards of bark fell onto the dusty patch of earth below. Its limbs were brittle and barren of any foliage.

Thick roots from each of the trees had invaded my grave. They were interlocked in an endless battle vying for possession of whatever corpse might have lain in this patch of earth.

The low burn of twilight painted a backdrop behind the skeleton trees of the forest in hues of deep violet and vermillion. Deep shadows crept toward me along the landscape.

I heard someone breathing hard. Was that my breathing? I finally moved within the small space of my shallow grave. White wisps of downy feathers glowed in a pile underneath where I lay. I hoisted myself up the three or so feet and took in my surroundings.

Deep inside the forest was this city of the dead. Ghost-white skyscrapers crowded around me in neat little rows. Faded inscriptions whispered forgotten names. Crooked old trees stood sentinel, their bare branches reaching towards the twilight sky. Beyond was a landscape of trees and who knows what else in the dimming light of day. I shuddered at the thought of what might have lain in the land outside this necropolis.

Was I dead? I don't remember dying. But then again, who does?

I kept to slow movements so as not to disturb any unsavory things that might lurk in the shadows. My dead eye had yet to find anything out of the ordinary, but who knows what happened on the way here.

Why couldn't I remember the place I was before?

I scanned the horizon one more time. Standing still is fine if you are a tree. I needed to find my way forward.

Then I saw him. I stared into the wiry feathered face of a raven. He stared right back at me, matching my intensity.

"That was quite a fall, my dear. Are you well?" He flitted between headstones until he found one to his liking a few feet from me.

"I don't remember any fall." But that would explain why I hurt. My lace-fringed shirt, vest, and trousers were dressed in the charcoal of ashes and some of the pale white feathers from my grave. I brushed them off before tightening the cross strap of my satchel and then my belt. The goggles on my head were loose, and I secured them.

All the while, I didn't take my one good eye off this creature.

"Where am I?" I was surprised by how harsh my raspy voice sounded.

The Raven's eyes lit up with a knowing intensity. "You are there. And I am here."

He hopped and fluttered to a new gravestone closer to me.

"What *do* you remember, little one?"

My stomach tightened. The only thing I could remember was the dream ... and ... I opened my mouth and almost let my name slip out before changing my mind. I thought better of giving this stranger power over me.

"Not much, I'm afraid. Did you see how I got here?"

I continued to brush at the ashes as I tried to figure out this odd little creature.

"Alas, no, I only just arrived here myself."

The hairs on the back of my neck tingled all the way through to my spine. Something sinister was lurking behind his innocuous-looking feathered face. I tried to remain calm so I didn't startle him.

"Why are you here?"

The Raven ruffled his feathers a bit and cocked his head from side to side. "To do what needs to be done. Whether I like it or not. Hurry on, little one."

I began to pace a bit, trying to look as if his presence didn't bother me. I turned and peered into the coming evening to look for my escape. As my focus came back toward the Raven, my dead eye finally woke up with a searing pain that felt as if it were on fire. And then I saw in perfect clarity—a crimson glow exploded around the Raven in the blood red hues of his aura. Within the ever-changing crackle of his aura, another figure towered over the forest with an unforgiving gaze that penetrated to my very soul.

I stepped back from him.

"*What* are you?"

The Raven seemed unfazed by my reaction. He hopped onto the gravestone right in front of me and stared at my good eye. Not with malice or fear, but with something else. Something blacker than his matted and mangey feathers.

"My dear Anna, we don't have time for silly games. I'm trying to save your life. Hurry on now."

How did he know my name? I hadn't spoken it.

"Save my life? We're in a graveyard. What kind of —"

"CAW!"

His screech almost deafened me.

"Look behind you, my dear."

I turned around slowly.

I saw the trees and the fading glow of the sun's last light. Then darkness. It was almost night, so that didn't surprise me. But there was movement within. A shifting. Very subtle. Very slow. But determined.

I faced the Raven again. He had a smug look about him. "What you almost see is evil without regret or remorse. It is coming for you. Hurry, we must."

"I'm not going anywhere with you. Whatever you are."

With false confidence, I strode away from the Raven. I made it only a few feet before a black tentacle evaporated the ground in front of me. I jumped backward. The throbbing of my dead eye was now matched by that of my heartbeat.

I changed course back towards the Raven, who landed on a gravestone near me. He looked up at me with one piercing eye.

"My dear, The Darkness Within will devour your soul and wrench every bit of life out of you one agonizing molecule at a time until you are nothing. I may not always be truthful, but I do keep my promises. And for this aspect of your journey, I have vowed to keep you safe."

"The Darkness Within. Within what?"

"Humanity."

As I was taking in the Raven's answer, more ground vanished near us. There was no time to ponder the significance of his reply right now.

The Raven's aura flickered to the warm fiery hues of vermilion. Looks like I wasn't the only one afraid now. He turned and flapped his wings. It made him appear twice as big. "We must leave. *Now.*"

My dead eye tingled madly. Danger was very imminent. Whatever this so-called raven was, he was not my priority right now.

I nodded my head slightly, and the Raven took flight.

I broke into a run to keep up with him. After only a few steps, I slammed into a headstone that split in two due to the force of my impact and its age. I stopped for a moment to get my wind back. A sharp glance behind me into the nothingness revealed no shallow grave, no trees. Nothing. It was as if the last few minutes of this new life of mine hadn't existed at all.

I forced myself to my feet and into a run just as three black tendrils crushed the gravestone I broke. I found my way to a more even path and followed the Raven as best I could. Even he appeared frightened by this shapeless monster with the deadly tendrils.

My dead eye burned hot, and I felt the rush of wind as the ground right behind me ceased to exist. I stepped up my pace, but I just couldn't muster up as much energy as I should. That fall that I don't remember must have taken more out of me than I figured.

"Hurry on, little one!" The Raven scolded me.

"I'm going as fast as I can!"

"Hurry on, or you'll be dead!"

I moved as fast as my bones let me and tried to catch up to the Raven. My demise was close, and that scared me; I didn't dare look back again. But if I was dead already, would it even matter?

My breakneck pace didn't last long. The Raven stopped just a short distance ahead of me. A thick grove of trees reached out like a tunnel over the rest of the path as far as I could see. I was puzzled, since he had just told me to pick up my pace.

Then I felt it.

I could go no further. There was nothing physically holding me back. It was as if I lost the desire to progress forward despite my adrenaline pumping and my dead eye vibrating with hot intensity. The goddess herself had paralyzed my body and rendered me inert.

I took a breath and tried to push forward. Nothing. I willed my limbs to move and again, nothing.

The Raven stared at me. "Well?"

"What?"

"Say the name so we can pass."

I was confounded. "What do you mean? What name?"

I thought the Raven was going to explode from my response. "You mean you don't know?!"

"No. What name?"

The Raven hopped back and forth as if pacing nervously. "I knew I shouldn't have agreed to this. I knew you weren't the one, and yet *she* insisted. Bah."

"Look, I don't know what kind of trick you're playing on me, but you said we needed to move and now I can't. How is this *my* fault?"

"Because, my dearest little Anna. If you are indeed who she *believes* you to be, you will know how to pass this gate into the next hour."

"And if I'm not?"

"Then you are as dead as the others buried under the embrace of the twin trees."

I thought for a moment about how many graves there must have been back there. Dozens? Hundreds? Some of them were very old. As if to reinforce the point, the hackles at the back of my neck pulsed as the Darkness obliterated more of our surroundings.

The Raven looked foaming mad now. "You need to name the guardian of this gate out loud so you can have power over him to open the gate! Now think, little girl, before I get really angry. I'm not planning on dying with a half-wit like you by my side."

But what name? The only name I remembered was mine. I closed my good eye. I felt a chill emanate from the pit of my stomach. My dead eye illuminated a glowing green object at my waist. I instinctively reached into my belt of useful things and pulled out the coin that had covered my good eye when I woke up here. It was warm, almost hot, and one of the inscriptions was glowing a vibrant emerald green. When I looked at it and tried to read the unfamiliar characters, A jolt of energy flowed through my veins and I heard a voice that was not mine say aloud words I couldn't remember forming.

"Behold, Khonsu, Lord of Luna, open the Netherworld that I may see my beloved Em. I am the Akh of prophecy. I am Anna. O all you gods and all you spirits be aware! Prepare a path for me."

I was stunned into submission, unable to move as I recovered. I had been possessed by a power I didn't understand so it could cast a spell in a language I had never spoken before.

My dead eye revealed a crystalline blue fire that lit the trees ablaze with its cold light. Within the sparkling snowflakes of energy vibrating in midair, I saw the ages-old god wave his hand to reveal the moon in the night sky. Luna shone her light down upon our path.

Trees singed by a spell of the old gods cracked and groaned as they were released from their duty.

I felt as if weights had been lifted from my body, and I was free to move again.

The moon fell from the sky and I heard the last remnants of the graveyard crumble into dust as I pulled myself to safety.

I stepped under the first trees and the black, bare branches lit up with a glow of leaves that illuminated the path before us. I was awestruck by the beauty of this orange tunnel. And was vaguely aware of the trees behind us collapsing inward upon themselves once more. I hoped that would give us some measure of protection ... for now, at least.

HOUR TWO : THE MEADOW

My sense of time unwound the longer we continued through the dense tunnel. The once-even-keeled path was overtaken by gnarled roots suffocating out any earth from under my feet. I felt as if we were going up a circular path even though my good eye told me we were traveling along more level ground.

Was it a few minutes that had passed? Hours?

The golden orange glow of the leaves burned out, leaving the Raven and I in the grip of this barren tangle of trees. My dead eye took up the slack so I could sense the path ahead. It showed me the wind carrying sparks of luminescent colors as they swirled around me in an ever-tightening loop.

The wind moaned its sorrow upon this narrow passageway. Had it been there the whole time? Its lament was getting louder with each step. The sensation of moving upwards in a counterclockwise motion got more intense as an azure and soft emerald glow blinded my dead eye.

One last step forward and I was on my back. Without falling, I found myself flat against the cold earth as it embraced my body. I was in the center of a small circle of scorched earth. Trying to sit up proved futile as dizziness forced me back down again. A burning smell lingered in my nostrils.

I stared up into the darkening canvas above my head. No stars yet. I watched the moon die in the graveyard. Was it gone here, too? Jagged blades of grass loomed large and framed in the velvet purple dome above me.

"Safety is not guaranteed, little one."

A mangy feathered face stared down at me. My head was pounding, but I was not going to let the Raven know it. His aura crackled a violent crimson color as I sat up to meet his gaze.

"What the bloody heck happened back there?"

The Raven cocked his feathered mane to one side and studied me for an uncomfortable moment.

"You really don't know, do you?"

"I know it was old magic. I know it came from me. But I didn't do anything. I was immobilized."

"My dear, if you can't explain it ... well, then neither can I."

I should have known better than to expect any kind of meaningful answer from him. The Darkness Within turned the graveyard forest into dust. And I did not want to get caught off guard again.

"Then at least tell me why you are helping me."

The Raven flitted closer and cocked his head from side to side. "Time reveals all, little Anna."

Feeling a bit better, I stood up slowly. We had landed in a meadow of grassland that stretched as far as both my eyes could see. As I looked over gentle slopes the field, I noticed shadows lurking within the tall waves of grass.

My dead eye ached with the auras of each person it discovered hidden within the shadows. The wind freed illuminated fragments of the soft emerald green auras that had been trapped on the blades of grass as they moved rhythmically in the wind. Those fragments looked an awful lot like the sparks I saw in the tunnel. A melancholy crept into my mood.

"What is this place?"

The Raven's aura shifted to the cooler tones of azure. He was about to tell me something real, for once.

"Whenever someone's dreams die, it shatters that person's soul. They wander here in the meadow, as the blades cut any lingering hope out of them piece by piece. Even the first of the fallen angels does not want souls once their dreams are gone."

I think I heard the Raven sigh. Why would he know about the first of the angels to fall from Heaven? And how would he know what souls the first of the fallen desires? I shivered a bit at the thought.

"Hurry on now, Anna." The Raven flitted off ahead of me.

I plodded along the ashes of grass and blackened dirt until a narrow path of an ancient, gravel road emerged. Stone markers etched in a long-dead tongue were scattered off to the side of the path along the way.

The blades of grass were a pale green with serrated edges of blood red. They taunted me with each step. The wailing I heard in the tunnel had subsided to a low hum at the base of my skull. It was a sound that I felt more than heard, a constant reminder of the sorrow permeating this place. The grass must was muffling the effects somewhat. Thank the goddess.

Where exactly were we headed? What was I so eager to get back to? I had a vague notion of a home that dissipates as soon as I tried to focus on it. Impressions of people I should have been able to remember were just beyond reach.

The Raven was right in my face.

"Pay attention, Anna. You almost drifted off the path."

My dead eye sensed no danger here other than the small creature in front of me calling itself a bird.

I matched his stare with my gaze.

"So what if I do?"

"My dear, once you step off the paved path, you'll never be able to find your way back. The grass shifts around the further you go into it. You will be forever lost like those wailing souls in the meadow."

"How long before The Darkness Within finds us here?"

The Raven found a perch on the remains of a wooden fence post. "I wouldn't know."

He clicked his tongue.

"Maybe this time, my dear, you will be better prepared to open the gate."

"What do you mean?"

The Raven's aura flashed the brighter crimson of anger. "Did you honestly think that was the only gate?"

It sounded like one of the stories I was told as a child. The one where a soul journeys across the night sky into the afterlife.

Maybe I really was dead.

Something familiar wafted in on the wind.

Muffled at first, but clearer with each step forward. A voice from my past.

"I'm sorry my dear, sweet child. I'm so very sorry."

"No, it couldn't be."

I was drawn to the sound of that voice. The one from my childhood. That soothing voice of someone close to me. Someone important.

My ... my grandmother ...

Why would she be here? That doesn't make any sense. She was a good and happy person. How could this have happened to her?

I have to know. The thought of my grandmother trapped in this meadow overrode any concerns of danger I might endure.

"Anna. You've gone off the path!" The Raven was too far behind me to catch up now.

The grass encircled me in an instant and even the slightest touch was like a razor against my skin, leaving tingling pinpricks. Each blade marked my skin with thin trails of blood, but I pressed on. My dead eye caught a glimpse the golden saffron tones of her aura wafting between the blades of grass. It was *my grandmother.*

I pushed back the tall grass, and it spread itself upon me unrelentingly as I continued toward her. I forced my small frame through the ever-thickening grass. I could feel my sense of time coming undone yet again. My only focus was on that voice. Those words she kept repeating.

"My dearest little one. I'm so very sorry."

What did they mean?

What ... was it again?

The words of ... that woman. A woman.

Who ... was repeating those words?

Someone ... I should know ...

The grass was slowly suffocating me as I stood there. I could feel the prickle of the blades constricting my body, make it harder to breathe.

I was on a mission to find some ... one? Some ... thing?

Maybe I should just lie down here for a while. It's been a long journey already. And there's certainly no better time to rest…

A flash of lightning.

Then, darkness.

The sky cries soft tears.

The burnt-out husk of a Queen Anne mansion looms high on a hill.

A girl weeps quietly in the shadows by the front veranda.

She starts to hum a melody as I approach. I can't quite place the tune, but it resonates within me like my own breath.

I go to place my foot on the first step when I'm ripped back to reality.

A withered branch had wrapped itself around my arm. My fingers tingled with pins and needles. Yet, my dead eye didn't sense danger. Upon closer examination, this branch didn't belong to a tree. It was pale, warm, and had fingernails.

The wailing wind whispered to me, "Anna."

The branch that wasn't a branch yanked me forcefully into a denser cocoon of grass. The blades were not sharp here and the wailing wind was a background noise that was easily tuned out. There was that familiar warmth from my childhood.

"Grandmother." She stood before me, just as prim and proper as I remembered. Not one strand of hair out of place.

I always thought her aura was so beautiful. Warm golden-yellow sunset tones with hints of orange radiated in calming waves from her tiny frame.

"Oh, my dearest Anna. I have missed you so."

Her smile radiated love. I went in for a hug and her embrace warmed my chilled bones. But she was quick to pull away from me.

"I haven't much time." She fumbled in her pocket for something.

Her clear blue eyes leaked a few tears around the edges. I gave her a hint of my smile. She pulled out a weathered copper ankh from her patchwork pocket. It was unlike any I had seen before.

"This old relic of mine will help you when you need it most. Goddess knows it has saved my life more than once."

The bars of the cross had tapered ends, and the loop on top was fashioned into an eye. Grandmother pressed it into my hands before I could get a better look at it.

She gripped my hands and stared into my soul.

"Anna, what you do here this night, this journey—is *your* sacred task to complete before the dawn breaks over the horizon. You must do it for *her* sake."

Grandmother held her stern but loving gaze on me.

"What *strange company* you keep these days, little Anna. One is the Darkness. One is the Light. She will make you choose between them before this night is over."

"Grandmother, what do you mean? I ... "

She pushed me away.

"Listen, Anna."

Her eyes clouded over as her body drifted back into despair. The fog of her fragmented soul began to overtake her. She tapped me ever so gently near the center of my chest.

A coldness radiated from the pit of my stomach. I blinked. And I was back on the worn path as if I had never left.

I didn't mean to cry, but a tear slid down my cheek. I savored it for a moment before wiping it away.

The warmth of my grandmother's protection was growing cold. I tucked her gift into my belt of useful things next to my coin. My dead eye glimpsed an emerald spark as the two trinkets touched before settling into their separate spaces.

I wonder who *she* might be.

What did Grandmother mean when she said I was traveling with the light and the dark? The foretaste of decisions not yet made weighed on me.

I saw the Raven circling above the meadow in an attempt to find me. Odd how such a creature would be so worried about me.

No, he is not worried about me. That makes no sense.

He *needs* something from me.

I felt my grandmother's love, even if it was only for a short moment. The only thing she wanted from me was to see me. Because she *loved* me. I could feel it in my bones. The comfort of her embrace. I had forgotten how much I missed her and her wisdom.

My grandmother had just been ripped away from me. She didn't deserve to be trapped in this meadow of broken dreams.

And what did the Raven want with me?

I pulled out the old copper ankh and held it between my fingers as I thought of my grandmother. The metal was warm in my hands, igniting my anger.

I could save her. I just had to tap into whatever it was that opened the gate in the graveyard.

The Raven wasn't going to be pleased.

I pulled out the coin and pictured my revenge in my mind's eye. Although I knew what I wanted, the words still echoed through me like I was channeling someone long dead. The energy of untamed magic blazed through my body as I prepared to release my anger upon the meadow.

"Ra, Lord of Sol, hear my voice! I call you to shine your light down upon this land and show it your truth. Make these souls whole again."

My dead eye revealed the white hot glow that lit the grass ablaze. Amidst the backdrop of the fiery meadow, I saw the shadow of Ra towering over the horizon as he cast his purity upon the land.

The Raven saw what I was doing, but it was too late.

"Anna, no! You will kill the both of us!"

My burning rage destroyed the deadly meadow of shattered dreams. It burned every blade of grass with the ferocity of a god gone mad. My dead eye showed me the auras of each soul exploding into a rainbow of color as the flames enveloped their broken bodies. The wailing that had assaulted my ears dissolved into a chorus singing in heavenly awe.

Every fiber of my being reveled in the euphoria of unbounded joy that filtered through me as each soul was freed. I felt alive, maybe for the first time in my life. And I knew that I would never be able to experience this kind of wonderment again.

I had done this.

I had saved these souls.

The sweltering heat of the fire bearing down on us pulled me back to the reality of my situation. But I didn't move.

"CAW!"

The Raven sideswiped me with his small body. His aura crackled and burned the deepest oranges of vermilion and bloodiest of crimson reds as he flitted and fluttered from one place to another.

"I won't let your journey end here, Anna. There's too much at stake."

"What do you want from me?"

The Raven swirled around me in a mad frenzy. "Nothing that you don't want for yourself."

We were trapped.

"Why are you helping me?"

"Because, little Anna, that is the only way forward."

Amid the raging inferno, the spark of a cool azure aura revealed by my dead eye confirmed the truth of the Raven's words.

The fire had completely surrounded us.

There was no place to go.

I had heard that if you died in a dream, you died in your real life, too. It was a silly notion, really. But what happened if you died and you were not sure if you were already dead or just dreaming?

HOUR THREE : THE SHORE

I had always been fascinated with fire. I loved how the flames danced in an endless pattern. A controlled fire was useful. But let it loose in anger, and it became a devastating force to be reckoned with.

The Raven singed himself again, trying to break free from the wall of crackling flames.

"What were you thinking, little one?"

The Raven's flickering vermilion and blood crimson aura was a perfect complement to the oranges and yellows of the meadow burning away its despair.

"Killing us is not the way to get the answers you seek, Anna."

He flitted about the perimeter of the fire, looking for any opening that would allow an escape. I remained calm.

"Come and sit on my shoulder, Raven."

"Are you insane?" His entire aura was the most vivid vermilion now.

"Come to me and you will be safe. What other choice is there?"

Behind his coal eyes, he thought for a long moment. Tail down, he swooped in and landed on my left shoulder.

"What now, little one?"

"We wait until the fire dies."

He cocked his head towards me. "I won't die today, little one."

"You won't as long as you stay put."

The flames teased us as they threatened to consume us like the meadow. The heat was unbearable. I closed my eyes and took a deep breath. All the anxiety left my body as I exhaled.

Amidst the fire's anger, something gave way—I felt it in my bones. Just like the gateway in the graveyard that let us pass into the tunnel.

When I opened my eyes, the fire was gone. All that remained of the meadow was scorched earth. Not a single blade of grass defied the devastation.

My head was clearer now. My anger evaporated into the dusk of the evenfall.

"Indeed, you are powerful, as was foretold. But how did you know the fire wouldn't burn you?" The Raven's aura lit up a cool azure darker than the midmorning sky.

I wasn't about to let him have the satisfaction of an answer. And I really didn't know myself. I just had a feeling that since I cast the spell, the fire couldn't hurt me.

With the grass gone and my grandmother's soul freed, my dead eye showed me a framed structure in the distance. It had a steeple in the center and the roof was a dark color that blended with the charred landscape.

I was drawn to it.

Not in the same way as when my grandmother found me, but still. There was something there I needed to see.

The Raven's claws dug into my shoulder as he whispered into my ear, "Are you sure that is the path you should take, Anna?"

I didn't say my desire out loud. My dead eye would have sensed danger if he tried to read my thoughts. But this is the second time I felt like he's reached into my mind. After all, he did know my name before I spoke it in the graveyard.

I gave the Raven a look and strode ahead confidently towards our new destination.

The building was still pretty far away. It was a holy place, from what my dead eye could tell. Radiating a rainbow of colors in a pretty little pattern, it was disturbing and comforting at the same time.

We had been traveling in silence since the burning of the meadow. My dead eye began to ache. The Raven sensed it too. I stopped to let my dead eye take in the whole landscape.

It was my good eye that caught it.

Our shadows were out of sync with us. Ever. So. Slightly.

The remains of the meadow crawled along with us. Blackened land beneath our feet mirrored my steps after I had taken them. It was more than just earth and shadows. I stood still and the Raven looked at me and then at my shadow as it caught up to me.

"Hurry on. Now, Anna." The Raven led the way, scouting for a safe spot ahead of me.

My feet grew heavier with each step. I was fighting gravity itself for each new movement. The earth beneath me turned into a viscous, grasping mire. My boots were bound up in black quicksand as my body gave in to its irresistible pull.

My dead eye lit up as it sensed the evil below me. Its aura was disjointed, like the tingly rainbow colors against the black of unconscious sleep.

Each movement was a battle against the relentless pull of The Darkness Within. I clawed at the gritty, damp earth. My body was dragged into its ever-tightening grip. My dead eye was pounding and sending the tingle of danger up and down my entire spine.

The dirt and rocks were gnawing at my face now, my body was useless. The claustrophobia of my suffocation overwhelmed me.

A torrent of images assaulted my mind.

A young woman who had an old face.

An old man who had a broken face.

A girl who felt dead in the waking world.

I watched as the young woman swallowed her sadness in a thousand small pills and lay down to a persistent sleep.

I witnessed distinguished older gentleman's entire body crack and crumble as he fell victim to fate's curse.

And the girl. Who was this girl? She stood silent and alone in a world that passed her by. She was invisible in her solitude. I felt a kinship with her.

All these people were so removed from me at this moment, and yet, so familiar. Despair engulfed me from my soul outward to the entirety of my being.

My body and my mind were in agony. My dead eye's vision no longer penetrated the earth and the blackness that engulfed me. My good eye was about all that remained free. It was no use to continue struggling.

I heard a muffled caw near me. The Raven was suffocating. His black feathers already melded with the darkness that was swallowing us.

Then.

Time.

Slowed.

In the stillness of the moment, I saw a blue-white light explode within the periphery of my dead eye's field of view. Twilight's cloak ripped open as this light streaked across the sky. The darkness of advancing night evaporated into the bright light of mid-day.

The Darkness Within shrieked in pain as the entire sky lit up with a bolt of lightning in slow motion. The shadow retreated into the pores of the earth and released me from its deadly grip.

The images faltered and shattered as the night terrors that had been thrust upon me against my will faded away.

I fought my way to my knees in slow motion.

Time returned to normal as I watched the light hurtle towards my destination. The small shrine in the distance and the blue light merged silently. A small explosion lit up the humble structure, and a few moments later, the after-shock hit me at full force, knocking me backward. The Raven was thrown down to the ground.

I forced myself upright on shaky legs. A bit of smoke and debris hung in the air as the twilight settled in once more, a bit grayer than before.

"Great, another lost cause to join our menagerie." The Raven's whispers drifted towards my ears.

"You know what that was?"

"Perhaps." The Raven grumbled from his weathered dull gray beak.

Whatever it may be, it had to be better than the quicksand death that nearly drowned out our lives.

We were close enough now to see the small octagonal building was nestled near a river. It was a shrine of the Sect of the Nazarenes. Its Byzantine cross stood strong atop a short steeple. The entrance was protected by ivy that had intertwined itself upon the wood and concrete facade.

The roof and walls on the one side where the lightning struck were a twisted mess of broken stone and wood. The windows that hadn't shattered glowed with a surreal illumination from inside that brought their stories to life on the stained glass.

"There's still time to move on, Anna."

I wasn't about to let the Raven talk me out of this. The tingle at the back of my neck and my dead eye was giving me a warning, but I chose to head toward the chapel anyway.

When I reached the front doors, I found they had been pushed off their frames. I stepped softly into the holy place.

"Hello, child."

Standing before me was the most beautiful being I had ever seen. Each change of light or blink of the eye and their gender, hair, and skin color morphed into another. Their clothes were simple garments that changed as frequently as their face. Their aura was every single color of the rainbow, plus gold and silver.

But their eyes remained the same color. A cold diamond stare that penetrated deep into my soul.

"We have been waiting a long time for your arrival, Anna."

A hint of sulfur lingered in the air between us. Wisps of smoke wafted up from blackened stumps on their upper back. White feathers, like the ones that covered me in the graveyard, drifted lazily down from the sky. "Do not be concerned. Our feathered appendages will grow back in due time."

"*What* are you?"

"We are the bringer of light." The words radiated through my body like rays from the sun.

"Some of your kind call us … Messenger."

I stood there for a long moment, basking in the glory of this holy being.

"So you found us, Angel." Squawked the Raven, his aura flashing vermilion and crimson behind his matted and coarse feathers.

The gorgeous Angel continued to look at me. It was as if the Raven was only a figment of my imagination. I was overjoyed because they deemed me worthy of any attention. It was as if my grandmother's love and warmth had been magnified beyond my imagination and saturated the very cells of my body.

The Raven flitted his coal colored form directly between me and the Angel. "Just because you saved us doesn't give you the right to gloat."

I shooed him away. Maybe now I can finally get some answers about what's going on.

"Where am I?"

They seem puzzled by my question. "You are where you are supposed to be at this moment in time."

"What am I doing here, then?"

"That which has been deemed your sacred duty."

I swear the Raven had a smirk on his face as I attempted to pry information from our new companion.

"Great, you speak in riddles just like the Raven."

"We speak the truth from a place beyond your understanding." The Angel strode past me and the damaged walls cracked and creaked in their wake.

"This journey makes no sense to me. I don't remember where I came from or why I'm here."

The Angel did not turn to face me, but their reply resonated inside my mind. "Did not your grandmother speak of the importance of your journey?"

"She did, but—"

They continued out of the shrine without another word. The remaining walls groaned as the Angel departed. I looked at the Raven and he looked back at me.

"Don't be so keen on shiny rainbow things, little Anna." The Raven hopped along beside me as we left the holy place behind us.

We were only a few paces from the shine when I the ground shook beneath my feet and heard a deafening noise behind us. I turned to witness the remains the shine heave and collapse upon itself. The once-proud cross fell from its perch into the rubble.

The Angel was at the shore standing stone-still—unmoved by the demise of the shrine. The dusty hues of the fading day desaturated the once-golden sand into a dull gray powder.

"Why are you helping me?"

The Angel's rainbow hues wavered and flashed in the cooler tones of azure and emerald for a moment. "I hold true to that which I have been consigned."

They stood upon the water not far out from the shore. Tiny ripples pushed away from each of their feet in deference to the pure being that trod upon its surface. They chanted a spell in muted tones as they stared off into the distance across the water.

The Raven seemed more agitated than usual. "You will have to make difficult choices ahead. I hope you are prepared."

"We will find out soon enough." I tried to sound as confident and convincing as I could.

Where the water met the sky, the curtain of nightfall parted for a heartbeat. A soft, warm glow appeared and floated closer to us.

A lone figure of a boatman came into view as he steered his fragile craft reverently toward the three of us. He was taller than the Angel and bone thin. Though he wore a thick cloak, I could see hints of a grotesque visage. My dead eye gleaned that something was not quite right, but I couldn't quite make sense of what I was seeing. It was as if his face was not his face. Or it was on backward. Or something.

He pointed his bony finger at my good eye before turning his hand over to reveal his open palm.

"Well?" Demanded the Raven.

"I-I don't understand."

The Angel answered as patiently as a perfect being could. "The Celestial Ferryman requires payment to carry you into the West."

"He can't have my good eye."

"Eyes are not the currency of the dead, child. A more lasting trinket is required." The Angel stared vacantly at me.

My dead eye saw what I had missed.

The coin. The one that was covering my good eye in the graveyard. It was glowing green at the periphery of my dead eye's vision.

I pulled it out of my belt pouch, and it was warm to the touch. The glow reverberated in time with my heartbeat. Each movement was slower than the last.

My body started to sway, and I could hear the Raven say something that sounded so far away.

"... spellcaster ... *is* ... payment."

It didn't really matter to me. I felt a relief, an unburdening of whatever life may have done to me.

My vision grew dark, but maybe it was just the night sky above. I was laid out on the weatherbeaten deck of the boat. My arms folded across my chest. I was moving so slowly that I couldn't recall if I put them that way or not. I felt the warmth of the silver coin laid deliberately and delicately over my good eye.

I was calm as my breathing slowed. It was like being lulled to sleep when I was a small child in my grandmother's arms.

Was this what dying was like?

HOUR FOUR : THE RIVER

A flash of lightning.

Then, darkness.

The sky cries soft tears.

The burnt-out husk of a Queen Anne mansion looms high on a hill.

A girl weeps quietly in the shadows by the front veranda.

She starts to hum a melody as I approach. I can't quite place the tune, but it resonates within me like my own breath.

I'm only a few steps away from the front veranda. I can see she has dark hair like me.

I place one foot on the stairs. The worn wood groans its displeasure under the pressure of my weight.

The girl turns to face me and I can see her clearly for the very first time.

I gasped for air as I realized I wasn't quite dead yet.

I was flat on my back and couldn't see out of my good eye. It took me a moment to recall that I was on the boat. My good eye was hot and I instinctively reached up to touch it. I pulled the metal coin from my good eye to reveal all the stars of the heavens looking down upon my insignificant self. The Celestial Ferryman hadn't taken my coin after all. I tucked it back into my belt of useful things.

Countless constellations of judgment glared down at me from the veil of midnight above. If only I could remember what I had done to have earned their disapproval.

"About time you awoke, little one." The Raven was perched on the edge of the boat near the bow.

The Angel stood near me, staring off towards our destination, indifferent to my waking.

I could feel the Celestial Ferryman staring at me for a long moment as he continued to row us toward the West. With deliberate strokes of his oars, he commanded the water to take us where he directed. His bone-thin arms were so powerful that the boat felt like it was floating upon the ether of the heavens.

The boat was larger than I remembered upon its approach. It was just the right size for our small complement. Just enough room to spread out a bit, but not so big the Celestial Ferryman couldn't control it with ease. Battered from many a storm weathered but still was surprisingly solid, despite an occasional creak or groan emanating from the old wood planks.

I sat there for a moment, pulling the pieces of this version of the dream together before it dissipated. The scattered fragments were already on their journey from my memory.

What I did remember didn't yet make much sense.

Whose house was that girl playing at?

That tune she was humming resonated deep within me. It must have been something I heard as a child.

And her face, it was... it was right there. I saw it, I know I did. And yet, it vanished as soon as I came back to consciousness.

Why could I remember a persistent dream better than where I came from? Or who my family was? I only remembered the bits that make *me* me at my core, but not much more.

How did I know magic?

Maybe the spellcaster isn't an object?

I got up and walked the deck of the small craft. I was so overwhelmed by the Angel that I hadn't noticed that the Celestial Ferryman did not have an aura. I had never met someone without the color of their aura to show me who they really were.

Usually, there is at least a hint of a color swirling around their body to give me some clue as to who someone is and what their intentions might be.

Is this how normal people feel all the time? No luminous aura colors, no heightened awareness of a dead eye to guide them along the way? Just a limited color view of the world in three dimensions.

I didn't like it. The not knowing.

I gazed into the river to soothe myself. My good eye only saw a distorted reflection of me staring back with dreadful malice. But my dead eye showed me a river alive with shifting aural colors pulsing just below the surface. Just like me, my reflection was split between two worlds.

Staring into the ripple's hypnotic rhythm on the surface of the water invoked an immense sadness from deep within me.

"What you see and feel are the tears of those left behind." The Angel faced me now, their diamond eyes staring through me.

"Their grief carries the soul to its final destination in the West."

"So I'm dead."

"That remains to be determined, child."

"Am I dreaming, then?"

"What are dreams but a form of death? You are ... somewhere between."

The Angel turned their gaze back to the horizon now, leaving my soul defeated.

I looked toward the Raven, and he nodded to me.

So... I wasn't dead. Yet.

I guess that was a comfort.

The Raven tilted his head toward the bow. It wasn't a large boat by any means, but up here, any conversation would be masked by the sound of the water and the Celestial Ferryman's rowing.

"My dear, I do feel it is my duty to tell you this: the Angel is not to be trusted."

"*You* are one to talk."

"Little Anna, sometimes we are trapped in circumstances beyond our control. It would be wise for you to remain mindful."

Strange. My dead eye showed no signs of deception from the Raven's aura at all. His crackling blood-crimson even calmed to a cooler azure shade for the briefest of moments.

"What is the spellcaster?"

The Raven cocked his head toward the horizon. "Some families are blessed by the gift of the Magnificent Toth. Their ancestors are woven into the fabric of the tapestry of the universe and send relics as guides or tools."

If only I knew what to do with them.

"Am *I* the spellcaster?"

He flitted in closer to me, and looked toward the Celestial Ferryman before speaking. "The spellcaster is potent in its power. It's your good fortune that only the dead are required to make payment in full."

The Angel pretended not to be listening, but was definitely closer than before. Their aura flashed vermillion for a blink of an eye.

The last burning embers of hope faded as twilight died out and the dark, cold cloak of night finished wrapping itself across the dome of the heavens.

I huddled up on a shabby seat next to the humble cabin and pulled out the relics I had collected so far. A coin made of pure silver that was warm to the touch. Markings I couldn't read. They must be spells. I was never any good at written spells. They could get so complicated.

Inscribed on the copper ankh from my grandmother was the same dead language that was also on the coin. Probably not a coincidence.

Grandmother handed it to me so quickly that I hadn't realized it was on a chain of pure silver. I wound it around my neck and tucked it into my top so it was hidden from view. I could feel a warmth emanating from within the tiny jeweled sigil and coursing through my body. I felt my strength and energy returning to me.

I held the coin close to my heart for a moment and when it neared the ankh, my dead eye lit them up with the emerald green glow of magic. I pulled them away from each other and the glow dissipated. Curious. So these seemingly unrelated items knew when they were near each other. Magic was so strange sometimes.

I looked back toward the Angel, who stood still staring out into the midnight veil over the water. Their beautiful rainbow aura was a comfort and a mystery to me.

I moved near the edge of the boat and lazily let my hand drift down into the water. My hand started to hurt almost immediately. I glanced down into a grotesque visage of horror. Mangled bodies all scraped and scratched at me, threatening to pull me under. I tried to wrench my arm free, but had no leverage.

The Angel was on top of me and yanked my hand out of the water in one graceful motion. I looked out over the now calm waters.

"Bloody heck." I held my injured hand with my good one as I looked to the Angel and Raven for answers.

The Raven flitted over to me and gloated, "The sadness of tears cuts through flesh like knives."

I glared at him for a long, angry moment and I didn't care what he was behind that feathered mask. He didn't back down on his gaze, but I thought I noticed a hint of admiration before he hopped away.

My dead eye usually warned me of even slight dangers. Some kind of magic must be working against it here.

The Angel was like a statue next to me. Their diamond eyes had a coldness now that chilled my entire body.

"Hold out your hands, child."

My body reacted to the command before my mind could even process the words. The Angel was holding both of my hands in their hands.

A flashback snapped into my mind's eye. It was that girl.

The invisible one The Darkness Within had shown me in the meadow.

Her small body was cracked open at her heart. Tears streamed from the hole in her chest. Her sorrow engulfed the entirety of her world. She saw nothing but the bleak landscape of aloneness.

I could sense her fear and anxiety overtake every fiber of her being. Dark shadows hung over her, even during the brightest of days.

The vision was over almost as quickly as it started.

I looked down to find my wounds were already healed.

"It is fortunate that you are of strong breeding. Blood is an aphrodisiac to the dead." My hands suddenly felt heavy as they dropped to my sides. The Angel left me and returned to their post.

I collapsed against the side of the boat and just sat there, dazed. Why did a vision from The Darkness Within invade my mind when the Angel touched my hands?

Maybe I'm laying out there in the world right now and this was my reckoning before I died of a broken heart?

But I'm not dead yet.

The myths spoke of true ankhs carved from the light of the Milky Way that had healing powers. I guess even a relic as powerful as a true ankh couldn't heal the past.

I felt something when I first put the copper ankh on... Grandmother. It was like her warmth. Her... love. That was a comfort when I needed it.

What was it she said about my journey?

Anna, what you do here this night, this journey—is your sacred task to complete before the dawn breaks over the horizon. You must do it for her sake.

How can that be when I didn't even remember why I was here or what I'm supposed to be doing? Who was this "her" she mentioned?

If only I had more time with Grandmother, maybe I could have gotten more answers.

What did she mean by the "strange company" I keep these days?

One is the Darkness. One is the Light. She will make you choose between them before this night is over.

I guess "the darkness" and "the light" were pretty obvious. But who was this "she" Grandmother spoke of? And why would she make me choose?

And why the bloody heck was I half dead and half dreaming?

My dead eye sent a gentle tingle down my spine. I looked up from my collection of mystical baubles and my head began to spin. Gravity was spiraling around me for a moment and then it returned to normal. Countless burning stars were shaken from their place on the ceiling of the night sky and fell as if they were snowflakes. I stood up and moved closer to the bow of the boat.

Everywhere I looked, I saw the stars' gentle descent into the river. I reached out my hand to one of the larger orbs. It halted for the briefest of moments just above my palm. Yet eons seemed to pass before it continued on through my hand and into the water below.

The night sky was cold and vacant now. The water below us had evaporated and been replaced by the brilliant stars that once seemed so high above our heads. We now sailed upon them toward the West.

"Caw. There is no going back now, Anna." Even the Raven appeared awed by this sight.

The Celestial Ferryman was rowing on as if nothing had happened. The Angel remained steadfast in their position, looking forward to our destination.

The river of stars flowed smooth and silent. No more sound of the lapping waves to comfort me. Nothing to hear but the burden of my soul and my heart beating in my ears like time winding down.

Nebulas, galaxies, and the whole of the universe lay below us in all their wonder. Rising up from the horizon of immortality, our destination was before us.

I stood dead still as my heartbeat stopped.

HOUR FIVE : THE CAVE

I would have panicked if I hadn't been so calm. Not having a heartbeat seemed like the most natural thing for me at that moment.

The landscape before us was blacker than night. Not even the light from a trillion billion stars of the universe could illuminate the mysteries within.

The massive amorphous shape mimicked the rhythm of my missing heart. Mountains shifted into rolling hills that changed into barren plains. It was tumultuous chaos. Yet I was at peace.

The Angel's voice throbbed inside my head. "The time for judgment nears, child."

"What does that mean?"

"All who journey across the river Styx must be judged." The Angel's aura remained steadfastly multicolor.

I didn't have a good feeling about this. But there was little time to ponder the implications. I watched the world before me remake itself with each heartbeat. *My* heartbeat. Mountainous peaks appeared to go upwards forever when they seemed so small and insignificant just moments before.

My dead eye registered bursts of violet and emerald as fertile organic matter was born, smashed into itself, and changed form. But it was of no concern to me.

The sight before me was intoxicating in its simplicity. Maybe it was because it possessed my heart. Either way, I found it seductive. I felt powerful.

The Raven flitted over to me.

"Be wary, Anna. Deception often hides itself under the cloak of truth."

"What is this place?"

"Caw. Only you can know what it is to you."

I mumbled some sort of agreement. Why can't I ever get clarity about my questions in this place?

The churning chaos was so close now. I could feel each beat as if my heart had never left my body. My dead eye felt odd but was not alerting me to any danger.

The event horizon of the pulsating landscape collapsed in on itself. What was once a frenzied paradox now appeared as a perfect pyramid, pure in its intentions and secretive about its ambitions.

A vibration resonated from its core that resounded within

my body, my soul, and my mind. My companions and I sailed effortlessly toward this newborn null pyramid.

I was so used to the nothingness boring a hole in my vision that seeing something blinded me.

I blinked, and I felt lighter. Freer than I have ever felt in my entire life.

The shimmering effervescence of my soul stood in an ornate grand hall.

A universe of constellations bound by the zodiac was inscribed in the finest detail on the cold dead stone beneath me. I found it interesting how small and insignificant it all was now.

The story of humans played out in the pictographs etched onto every square inch of the marble walls. The rise and fall of countless civilizations sprawled across entire sections. Yet, amongst the chaos were tender moments. Lovers embracing under a starlit sky, hands clasped in friendship across cultures. It was a terrible, violent story filled with love and compassion. It was messy and raw and perfect.

There was no boat.

No Celestial Ferryman to guide us.

No Raven.

No Angel.

I was alone in this place.

Before me lay an incredible feast of nearly every kind of food imaginable. Delicacies from around the world adorned a long mahogany table in the middle of the room. A carved floral motif decorated the table. Delicate roses intertwined with exotic orchids, while humble daisies nestled alongside majestic sunflowers.

I glanced down to see my bones and flesh lying crumpled on the lapis lazuli floor.

Unbound from my mortal coil, I cared not for such earthly things. I had moved on.

I moved towards the large golden door at one end of the massive chamber. Dueling fireplaces larger than our boat lit and warmed the space with little effort. The door was maybe 30 or so feet tall and ornately carved with the genealogy of the sacred gods of old.

The giant doors welcomed me into the gilded hallway beyond lit only by torchlight. It reminded me of the orange tunnel of trees we passed through on our way from the graveyard. This time, though, the path was straightforward and unwavering.

The torches flickered and dimmed as I got further into the hallway. It was nearly pitch black except for the last embers of sunset lighting my way forward.

I stumbled in the blackness as the warmth of the grand hall gave way to a bitter chill I felt within my soul.

Fears from my mortal self tried to bleed into my soul and tell me to turn back, but I was no longer in a place to fear anything. I had to know where this passageway would take me.

I stepped from the hallway into the graveyard where I first landed.

"Bloody heck."

I turned to look behind me, and the ornate hallway was gone. I was back at the beginning again.

Twilight burned along the horizon just as I remembered. But something was different this time.

Underneath the two intertwined trees beside the grave where I woke up, silhouettes clustered together in their grief.

A tall, gangly man dressed in black, save the white collar gripping his throat, spoke words from the holy book of the Nazarenes.

A trio listened solemnly in their sadness and bowed their heads in reverence at the prescribed times. When the priest was done saying what needed to be said, the group lifted their heads.

The tallest one was an older man with gray around his temples. Next to him was an older woman whose once vibrant red hair color was dusted with age.

And there, between them, was a little girl who looked sad and confused. I couldn't quite make out her features, but she felt very familiar.

Why were they at the exact grave I fell into?

Was this ... my family? Was this the future ... the past?

A dream from another lifetime?

I peered into the grave that was once my grave, but not really. A small wooden coffin rested at the bottom of the hole carved in the earth.

The echo of my dead eye screamed at me as I nudged open the lid.

There, laid out on the soft velvet cloth was a body with my face. But it wasn't quite my face. There was something sinister about it. A darkness I couldn't quite place.

What was going on?

The family—my family?—turned their backs on the empty vessel down in the ground and abandoned the dead girl in the coffin. Their destination was just outside the rusted wrought iron border separating the living from the dead.

They were walking up to the same burned-out Queen Anne house from my recurring dream. But here, in this time and place, it was only starting to show its age with weathered gables and muted dirty paint tucked behind an untamed landscape. The fire was biding its time to devastate the lives of this sullen family.

"Deception often hides itself under the cloak of truth." I heard the Raven's rasp ringing inside my mind just before we, I, entered the oblivion of the pyramid.

Maybe this was all a dream within a dream.

The family entered the broken-down old house, and they left the front door open. Were they expecting me?

I approached the stairs just like in my dream.

Then the humming began. The melody that haunted me with each version of my dream invaded my mind from all sides. No longer a phantom from my childhood, it was now a piercing tune that became more excruciating with each note.

I held my gaze on the open door. From the shadows, a pair of crystalline amethyst eyes glared back at me. The door slammed shut.

The windows in the house all shattered in a flash of lightning that ripped open the sky. Shards of sharp glass rained down on me as the house started to burn out of control. I slumped to the splinted veranda and began to weep uncontrollably.

I lay exposed and vulnerable, crying without remorse. I had lost my family.

I was lost.

"Welcome back, my dear." The Raven's grizzled beak and beady little eyes greeted me once more. I felt the familiar motion of the boat against the water underneath me.

I wiped the sadness from my good eye. My head was throbbing.

No, not my head. My heart was back inside my chest.

I never realized how loud my heartbeat was until it was taken from me. I gave myself a moment to adjust to the vibration of my heart's rhythm again.

Still, something wasn't quite right. I was back in a body. Not entirely sure it was *my* body. My dead eye didn't feel quite right. And my limbs seemed out of proportion. I raised my hand and tried to wiggle my fingers. My movements were sluggish and uncoordinated. I touched my face, and it felt unfamiliar but not uncomfortably so.

"You don't seem quite like yourself, Anna," The Raven whispered coarsely in my ear.

The Angel graced me with their presence. "Hiding behind a mask will not hide you from your truth, child."

It wasn't just me, then. Both the Raven and the Angel could see that this was not the same body I started my journey with. It was a near-perfect replica of my body and was mostly comfortable, but still awkward around the edges. I steadied myself and stood up as best I could. My toes tingled strangely, and my legs were shorter than I recalled.

My dead eye felt muted. But I didn't need it to tell me something was not right. Lanterns illuminated the striations of geological time along the walls of the cave. The stillness of time engulfed me.

The Celestial Ferryman was next to me in an instant. With an exhale, he wrapped his thin limbs around my body and confined me in his grasp before I could comprehend what was happening.

His cloak fell away to reveal a prison of worn ivory bandages enveloping me. I thrust the back of my head into where his face should have been.

"Bloody heck." I yelled in pain as the sharp crack of something breaking rolled through the cavern. My head hurt, but didn't feel damaged either. I tried to get a better look, only to discover the Celestial Ferryman's face wasn't where it was supposed to be. It was a contorted mask of what appeared to be a man in agony. The shattered pieces slid off the back of his head and onto the deck.

The Angel's voice thrummed inside my skull. "He Who Looks Behind is doomed to peer only into the past while binding those to be judged so they may face their future."

"I did try to warn you." The Raven cocked his head and ruffled his feathers. I couldn't quite make out the Raven's aura. But I felt his smirk for the briefest of moments before flitting off to the front of the boat.

I attempted to wriggle loose from my mostly mummified state, but He Who Looks Behind stood firm in his grip on me.

The constant vibration of the Angel's aura between different shapes and colors had ceased. They had settled on a solitary physical appearance, for now, I guess. It was a nice break from the constant shifting of personas. They directed their intensity toward me as the boat came to a standstill in the water. "This is an ill-fitted body for you, child."

The only sound was the dripping of water from the stalactites and the pounding of my heart.

A new voice reverberated throughout the cave.

"I am Ma'at, Bringer of Order and Balance. I will render justice upon your soul. Only I can see the *truth*. You are imperfect. Flawed. A *disgrace*."

I tried to ignite the same rage that let me burn the meadow, but nothing happened. I know I was angry, but this new almost-body of mine did not let me actually feel it.

"I have witnessed your soul laid bare."

I tried to focus on the coin like I did when I opened the gate. Instead, a chill snaked its way up from deep within me.

"I have stripped you of your fragile body."

My not-quite dead eye throbbed in time with my heart's pounding.

"I have weighed your heart."

This can't be good. I didn't know what else to try.

"Bloody heck." An ostrich feather floated down from above and landed on the water next to us without making a single ripple.

"You are not ready for The Field of Reeds. It is not yet time for this soul of yours to dwell in the eternal pleasures."

He Who Looks Behind released his hold on me, and I felt the balance of my scales shift. The river and boat beneath me gave way to emptiness below. My stomach lurched into my throat as we were cast down into the depths of the abyss.

HOUR SIX : THE NECROPOLIS

We fell into complete darkness. Time lost its meaning. Seconds lasted an eternity. Air rushed past my ears and gave a sense of motion, but the absence of light was so complete it was like I was standing still.

I would have screamed if I could have caught my breath.

I heard the Raven trying to orient himself so he could fly properly. The Angel was silent in their fall from the light above.

If only I had my dead eye to see their auras right now. As it was, my not-really dead eye showed me fuzzy splotches of color in random patterns.

Right side up or upside down. I suppose it didn't really matter in the absence of light.

I was dizzy and felt sick. Of course, my body was not quite my own, either.

It didn't help that I was drenched by the river as we started our sudden descent.

Falling forever was terrifying until it was boring. The anticipation of a landing that never comes and my mind began to wander.

Was the ground inches a way? Miles? Maybe it was years from me?

I couldn't help but think of the irony of it all. Falling to my death in a dream in which I will never wake. Or was I falling through my dream in a death that I will never know?

Of course, reality hit just when I started thinking interesting thoughts.

I had grown so used to falling and being soaked through that the danger of drowning hadn't dawned on me until now. The air had suddenly become viscous. The shock of submersion jolted me from my stupor and with a desperate kick, I realized I was swimming. I gasped for air as I surfaced in an azure pool in a small cove.

It took me a moment to coordinate these nearly identical limbs the right way to get me to the shore.

The Angel hovered a foot above the water. Their eyes were focused on something other than my near drowning.

I dragged myself onto the beach and dry heaved—the acrid taste of bile burned in my throat. My fingers sunk into the gritty, ash-colored sand as I tried to calm myself. So, not dead yet. We were now inside an oppressively claustrophobic cave.

The Raven's grizzled feathered visage was in my face.

"First I almost died by fire. Now by water. I certainly hope you are worth all this trouble, little Anna."

"Me too."

I brushed the moist grit off my weatherworn leather trousers as I stood up. Even though we were further underground, there was no lack of light. Old gods bound in stone were holding up the walls, stoic and uncaring. Offerings from long-dead acolytes burned for all eternity in ornate braziers at their feet. The air was oppressive with the weight of countless centuries.

A steady, primal rhythm pulsated throughout the cavern and my body. The walls around us seemed to undulate with a life of their own, expanding and contracting in a slow, hypnotic pattern. A sickly sweet, musky odor permeated the air.

Was it me or were the walls breathing? I opened my mouth to ask the question but thought better of it.

"The Necropolis." The Raven shuddered.

"No one escapes from the venomous jaws of the Devourer of the Dead."

"But I'm not dead yet... right?"

"*You* are not. But the body you wear has been dead for quite some time now." The Raven's feathered face showed relief in light of this revelation.

"What does that mean?"

"Caw. Everyone makes their choices in life, little Anna. They must be prepared for the consequences." The Raven's aura flashed azure as his gaze settled on the Angel for a moment.

The Angel strode confidently past us, and the granules of sand quaked beneath their feet.

Great, that's just my luck to lose my real body and end up in a used one that has expired.

Both my eyes were throbbing. The coin sparked in my dead eye's vision from its safe spot within the small pouch on my belt of useful things. The white color of the beach seemed to glow as its granules submitted to the weight of my ill-fitted new body.

I was trying to concentrate on walking, but it was slow going. I fell to my knees and took a deep breath. I pictured my grandmother and allowed her calming presence to wash over me.

The sands shifted under me. I stood up as best as I could. My new legs were still too heavy and each of the billions of grains started to trap them. I tried to run, but it was too late. The sand writhed around my legs, and hands were grasping at my calves. I looked down to see two bony hands form around my legs and hold me in place.

The Raven responded by swooping in to try to assist. The entire shore was alive and was transforming to become hands, arms, and heads. The sand was coalescing into broken people. Some were just bones, some were lumps of flesh and bone, and others were horrific shambles of what used to be humans.

The Angel continued on their path as if they couldn't hear my struggle.

The Raven was pecking at the two bony arms gripping my legs as more hands thrust from the ground to take their place. He was promptly overwhelmed.

Ten thousand armies rose up from the shore and surrounded us. The hands holding me in place tossed me off of my feet as a headless body rose up from the ground to stand with its brothers and sisters.

Each of the shadows moaned and pleaded for mercy. Some turned to me with their pleas. They reached out and suffocated me as they begged for a way to escape a fate I hadn't determined.

I heard a sullen wraith of a man gasp, "Was what I did so wrong that I deserve such torment?"

The horror unfolding all around me was definitely *not* the work of The Darkness Within. Something else was going on here.

I fell forward and kept going as my world upended itself. I reached out into space, hoping to grab something solid. The hands holding me released their grip as bodies tumbled over each other.

The walls undulated with more ferocity. The entire cave floor became uneven, and entire sections became almost vertical. With each expansion and contraction, victims screamed and cried as they were tossed into the pit. Fire and brimstone brewed below us as the sinners were consumed by the fire in droves. The putrid stench of burning flesh overwhelmed my nose.

I had nothing to hold on to and was headed for the same fate. The Raven was tumbling with me and the Angel was nowhere to be found. I could feel the fires licking my face in anticipation. I tried to remember a spell, any spell that might help. But my mind was blank and my almost-body was not cooperating.

A million dead reached out to try to rip my soul from my body on their way to damnation. I said a small prayer to the goddess.

The torrent of mangled bodies streamed over me, clawing and grasping for anything to delay their punishment, even for a moment longer. I was assaulted on all sides, and I couldn't hold my grip any longer. My fingers started to slip from my precarious perch. I held my breath and closed my eyes in anticipation as I slid from safety into my fate.

Just as the rage of the inferno was about to embrace me with its angry flames, the cave coiled itself back down to a level position once more. My face stopped a few short inches from the furnace at the center of the cave.

"What just happened?!"

"Caw." The Raven landed gently on my shoulder.

"These souls have been condemned to endless torture. Ammit devours them whole only to regurgitate them again; repeating the cycle until the end of days."

Did I see an actual tear in the Raven's eye?

"And you, Angel, why didn't you help? With your powers, you could have easily saved not only me and the Raven, but all those souls, too."

"Judgment is not ours to make, child." The Angel's diamond eyes glared at the Raven as they spoke. Their rainbow aura shifted to blood crimson and back again.

White grainy ash polluted the corridor, a ghostly fog reducing visibility to nearly nothing. It fluttered down on us like snow. The gritty mixture clung to my skin and clothes.

No, not snow.

Sand.

White sand.

The Angels' rainbow aura shimmered between the flecks. "Born of dust, the wretched souls were trodden upon in life. Now they are ground down to dust again and again in the endless circle of their deaths."

The white, gritty remnants of the cursed souls continued to fall and coat us quietly in their sins.

"We cannot idle ourselves grieving for souls lost, child."

The Angel and the Raven looked at me expectantly.

I closed my good eye so I could focus. My almost dead eye humored me with glimmers of green on the coin. Parts of the inscription across the two bands along the outer rim of the coin shone faintly.

I pulled the coin from my belt of useful things. It was dead cold as I wrapped the warmth of my hand around it, wishing for it to work. I felt movement and my dead eye saw the bands rotating slowly as if unsure how to line up the right runes for a spell.

And then nothing happened.

No voice from within.

No spell pulled from my subconscious.

Not even a tingle of magic within my veins.

"Are you sure you are the Akh of the prophecy, child?" The Angel turned their back on me.

"Have faith, little Anna." The Raven whispered.

I set my vision toward the hellfire that had incinerated so many already. It seemed so real. The heat made my skin flush. Hypnotic oranges, reds, and purples danced across my vision.

The Angel waited. Neither impatiently nor patiently.

If I was already dead, then walking into the fire wouldn't mean much. If I was dreaming, then walking into the fire wouldn't hurt me.

What did I have to lose, then? I was supposed to be the Akh of the prophecy after all.

I took a deep breath. I remembered my grandmother and the gifts I received on this journey so far. I stepped toward the flames.

As I crossed the threshold, the flames changed from warmer hues to cool blues and purples. The cold chill of death burned deep into my bones as I crossed into the depths of the underworld.

Echos of the dead haunted this part of the cave, never quite dying but never quite alive either.

Regrets.

Requests for forgiveness.

Sorrow.

Anger.

Names of loved ones.

The real torture here was all the wasted lives. Time freely given and easily discarded as worthless.

My eyes welled up with tears.

"All these poor souls."

The copper ankh was pulsing with energy, trying to infuse me with strength, but I was too overwhelmed by grief. I clenched my fists to try to stem the flow of sadness leaking from my good eye.

The Raven perched on my shoulder gently as we traversed the serpentine path before us. Down and down we marched in concentric circles. I got lost in the vertigo of the damned as we continued to spiral.

The monotony of the fates of these sinners numbed me. My impetus to act was bored out of me and lost amongst the burnt dust of the shadows of people on their final pilgrimage.

There was no more hope. We were in the center of despair.

The weight of the sinners' trespasses fell upon my body, and I collapsed to the ground. The Raven held firmly onto my shoulder. The Angel stood in stoic silence.

I wept. Not for me. But for those who couldn't.

The Raven's little claws dug into my skin, drawing a slight hint of blood. "Hurry on, little Anna. Heavy is the cross born on the backs of those who live. Lingering in the Necropolis is not wise."

The world shook violently again, such that I was thrown flat on the ground and the Angel and Raven were tossed out of my sight.

"*You* do not belong here."

One of the old gods peered down upon me, frowning his disapproval. He looked majestic in all of his adornments of godhood, and I didn't care.

I had succumbed to the intoxication of this poisonous death. My almost dead eye was not powerful enough to distinguish a real threat from the sullen souls just existing in this pitiful place.

I still didn't feel right in this body. I tried to stand up but couldn't. I lay in the gravel of crushed souls, exhausted.

"*You* have stolen this body from another."

"I did no such thing. It was a gift from the goddess, Ma'at herself." I couldn't see the Angel or the Raven. All I could see was an old god about to render justice upon my weary soul.

I tried to grasp my ankh, but I was too tired.

"Hurry on, now, Anna."

The Raven cried weakly from the shadows.

I made it to my knees only for them to buckle under me.

"Hurry on, now Anna."

His rough voice was stronger already. But it didn't work on my broken spirit or my fractured new body.

I closed my eyes and waited for this old god to end my new-to-me body and my old soul.

"Get up, Anna!"

The Raven screeched at me one more time.

I wanted to move, but started to drift into unconsciousness instead.

"The time is now, child." The Angel's voice permeated my being and filled me with joy for the briefest of moments.

A spark within me awakened my real dead eye. It came to life once more and illuminated my ankh and coin. The copper ankh's energy surrounded me with a shimmering emerald aura. My blood pumped vibrant magic throughout my body.

A different set of inscriptions on the coin were overflowing with the emerald green aura of magic. I looked at the markings as they were revealed to me. Strange words from a dead language were spoken with a voice that was not mine from a body that most certainly did not belong to me. This body hummed with the energy of my ancestors as they cast their incantation.

"Osiris, Resurrector of the Dead. I command you to raise me up. For I am Anna. The body I inhabit is false, a tribute from Ma'at, the Judge of All Souls. The gods have been warned of my coming. My path is clear. Not even Death will stop me on my journey. Return me to my own self."

My dead eye revealed a turquoise fire that lit up the cavern and burned Ammit, The Devourer of Souls, from the inside out. The cavern trembled with his screams as Osiris ripped open his scaly hide with one hand. With his other, he flailed the serpent's body into submission.

The last thing I saw was Osiris reaching down to pick me up with his bloodied hands before I fainted dead away.

HOUR SEVEN : THE TOWN

A flash of lightning.

Then, darkness.

The sky cries soft tears.

The burnt-out husk of a Queen Anne mansion looms high on a hill.

A girl weeps quietly in the shadows by the front veranda.

She starts to hum a melody as I approach. I can't quite place the tune, but it resonates within me like my own breath.

I place one foot on the stairs, then another. The worn wood groans its displeasure under the pressure of my weight.

The girl turns to me and another flash of lightning reveals her face is my face.

I fall backward off the stairs into the mud below.

"Emma."

I sat upright in a bed I don't remember going to sleep in. I was in a room that was not mine. My arm was still outstretched toward the fading embers of my recurring dream.

My trusty dead eye lit up a twisted crimson around the Raven at the foot of my bed and a strange vermillion aura outlined the Angel standing by the window. Prickles crept down the back of my neck.

The Raven noticed I was awake, and he flitted over to perch on my footboard. His feathers were soiled with soot.

"You. Are. Awake."

Was the Raven talking stranger than normal?

"You. Are. Prey."

"What are you jabbering on about?"

"You. Tried. Deceive. Me."

The black of the Raven's feathers dripped off of him to reveal white matted feathers underneath. I looked up to see the Angel with full, black wings looming over me.

They spoke to me with the unity of a voice from the depths of the shadows.

"You. Tried. Hide. River. Stars. Underworld. Fail."

The shivers ran up and down my spine as I lay paralyzed in my bed.

"You. Body. Died. Tasted. Soul."

I closed my good eye hard and tried to wake up for real this time, but I couldn't. I tried to push the crackling rasp out of my head.

"You. Body. Clever. Double."

I reached up to touch my grandmother's copper ankh. Her love's warmth washed over me. The tendrils oozing from the Raven started to crawl up my skin.

"You. Die. Before. Wake."

I kept my good eye shut and my dead eye showed me my coin glowing a soft emerald color in my belt of useful things. The eyes on both sides of the silver disc glimmered with the emerald energy of magic.

"She. Kill. You."

The white Raven was three times as large now. The dripping tendrils of his black husk were wrapped around my throat, choking me.

The Angel's dark mangled feathers entangled me in their vise grip.

My throat closed up. My breath was almost gone. My body started to go limp as I tried to cast a silent spell upon both relics.

The pressure released from my throat as my dead eye revealed the Raven's familiar crimson red aura.

I heaved and gasped as I blinked my good eye open. The nightmare wrapped around my dream was over for now.

"Better, little one?" The beady eyes and midnight black feathers of the Raven were almost a comfort to me.

"I-I think so." My voice was still rough from my struggle.

All that was left of the white Raven's assault on my dream was the sweat dripping from my face and the bruise on my neck. My arms moved smoothly to wipe some of the sweat from my forehead. I wiggled my fingers. These were my fingers once more. I took a deep breath and felt the truth of it circulate through the entirety of my being. The awkward replica of my body was no longer. I was back in my rightful place.

"Your recovery should be imminent as you have returned to who you were, child."

If only I could remember exactly who I was in the first place. The wingless Angel illuminated the room from their place near the grimy window.

"It's not that," I croaked.

I freed myself from my sweat-soaked sheets and hoisted my legs over the side of the bed. We were in a confined, sparse room with little furniture. Just the bed and a solitary, tattered-fabric chair by the window. The dingy, water-stained wallpaper was cracked and peeling.

"The Darkness Within ... It spoke to me. It knows where we are. And it is *not* happy."

The Angel simply strode out of the room, their aura lingering behind them.

The Raven hopped in closer to me. "Ma'at gave you the wrong body in the cave on purpose."

"But why?"

"The gods do like to play with their toys." The Raven stared at me with his little black eyes for a long moment.

"To hide me. Or to hurt me?"

"Caw. Who can fathom the immortal, little one?"

The Raven flitted over to the windowsill.

"We must hurry on, Anna. Time is winding down for us in this place." The Raven ruffled his feathers a bit before shaking them back to normal.

I pushed myself out of bed and tried to stand. Even though I was back in my own body, I was still unsteady on my feet. The floorboards protested with loud groans. I staggered over to the windows.

I looked down from our second-floor windowsill onto a weathered scratch of an old town carved into the desert. The buildings, a patchwork tapestry of unbleached adobe and worn wood, were huddled together, seeking shelter from the unforgiving expanse of the endless horizon. The hum of electric lights buzzed in the air as the small, round bulbs bathed the unpaved street below in a sickly yellow light.

The Raven twitched his head from side to side as he watched the people below. "Hell hath no revenge like Purgatory."

A few folks were on their way somewhere at this ungodly hour of the perpetual dawn. No auras seemed to register with my dead eye.

"Caw. Wherever they try to go, they always end up back here."

As I turned to leave, I saw an older woman with once-vibrant red hair now dusted with age. She reminded me of the woman from my vision in the cave. She gazed up at me with the purest azure eyes I had ever seen. I felt that familiar warmth of family. Could she be—

"Hurry on, Anna."

The Raven flew out of the room.

We caught up with the Angel in the street, heading east.

"Where did she go?"

I looked to my left and to my right.

"Be careful of what wishes you make, child." The Angel's voice throbbed in my head like a migraine.

She tried to blend into the crowd as she fled. I sprinted toward her, my heart filling with hope as my heartbeat thundered in my ears. I was focused on closing not just the physical distance, but that of time and loss that separated us.

People parted for me as I raced to see if this woman was who I thought she was. First, Grandmother was in the meadow. And now, here, my long-dead mother might be just a few paces away from me. I have to help her if I can.

"Anna, wait!" The Raven's raspy warning faded upon my ears and I raced onward.

My dead eye was pounding and I couldn't tell if it was because I was exhausted or if danger was near.

I was distracted and didn't notice the woman had turned sharply to face me. I stopped as quickly as I could, but I almost ran her down.

"How you've grown, little one."

Her blue eyes lit up with the same warmth as my grandmother's.

"Mother?"

My dead eye revealed her emerald and vermilion aura wafting upon the breeze in wispy tendrils from her body. It *was* her. Yet it wasn't entirely her.

Only possessed humans leak auras.

She reached out and held both my hands in hers. I was home again. I felt the joy of my childhood and basked in it as long as I could.

"I'm so very sorry I left you. I-I hope that one day you might forgive me."

Tears streamed down the sides of her pale cheeks as she embraced me. I held back my own stream of sadness. What was before me was only a shadow of the woman who was my mother.

"I was spared the underworld by the grace of your grandmother. But this Purgatory with no exit might as well be Hell."

She cast her soft eyes toward the ground.

"Let me help you, Mother. I freed Grandmother from the meadow."

"There's no time … take this before *she* finds us."

My mother slipped something cold and metal onto the ring finger of my left hand.

"Before who finds us?"

"With this ring, no one can ever take your heart and soul ever again, my love."

I could feel her being possessed once more by The Darkness Within.

"I love you, Anna. Remember that you loved her once—"

Her eyes glazed over as The Darkness Within consumed her entire body. Her aura faded away from my dead eye's vision.

"No, no, *no!*"

She was pulled away from me by tendrils that extended from the shadows lurking just beyond the electric lights' radiance. She convulsed into a more rigid stance.

"*You* cannot leave."

A voice came from my mother that was definitely not hers.

I felt the pit of my stomach freeze. We were blocked in by a small crowd of townsfolk that had gathered. I couldn't see the Raven or the Angel.

"You cannot *hide* any longer."

A woman's voice, warped by the dull intonations of dozens of possessed souls, enveloped me. My captors were all bound with wrinkles of black soot that oozed along their skin. They spoke as one.

"And now *you* are mine."

Tendrils started leaching from each body. They writhed and intertwined near me and around me, coming ever so close. But something was keeping them at bay.

"Who are you?" I stared directly into the now vacant eyes of my mother. I felt the warmth of my ankh and the ring as I focused on the coin with my dead eye.

"I am *us*," snarled the darkness that was once my mother.

"Are you Emma?"

The name from my dream-within-a-nightmare came to my lips without me thinking.

"I am a *goddess*."

My mother's once elegant frame contorted into a silhouette of a winged beast of a woman with a spiky feathered crown that reached for the heavens.

"You will know my *wrath*, Anna."

My dead eye saw the violent blood crimson aura of Emma's hatred pulsate from everything The Darkness Within had infected. I felt the heat of her rage as she shattered my mother's body with a sickening crack of bone and flesh.

My dead eye saw my ankh, the ring, and the coin spark emerald. I felt the tension relax within the town, just as it had at the other gates.

My mother's broken body collapsed upon itself onto the dirt road. I fell to my knees and gritted back my despair.

I just had my mother returned to me. Now she was taken from me again. And I didn't do anything to stop it. What good are all these long-lost spells trapped within me if I couldn't use them to save my family?

The flood of my sadness welled up within me, but I held it back. I didn't care if Emma is a goddess or even *the* goddess, I wasn't going to let this creature beat me.

I looked deep into the warped visage of Emma but found no answers there. My dead eye throbbed. The back of my neck tingled to warn me of the danger on all sides.

An army of citizens devolving into The Darkness Within tightened their circle around me. Black oozing tendrils threatened me no matter where I looked.

My anger erased my fear as I stood ready to take on this creature who just took my mother from me.

The sickening sound of bones cracking echoed across the plains as The Darkness Within extinguished the lives of the remaining townsfolk.

Mothers crushed to a pulp.

Daughters pulverized into dust.

Fathers reduced to grains of sand.

Sons obliterated into particles.

These souls who sinned in moderation were cursed into the shadows of the void for no good reason.

My grief and anger surged within me.

The Darkness Within raged in shifting shapes of discord as the souls it had devoured tried to escape. Multicolor hues of vaporous auras steamed off the creature before dissipating into nothingness. In the end, only the darkness remained as one amorphous wall of swirling shadows that trapped me in the long-dead town of Purgatory.

HOUR EIGHT : THE CROSSROADS

My wrath smoldered inside of me. I focused my dead eye on the coin of spells held tightly in my hand. I hoped it would reveal any spell to match my feelings. The ankh and ring sent reassuring vibes of warmth through my body, reminding me of their protection.

The Darkness Within stood before me, tendrils at the ready. It had threatened me in my nightmare and here, in this waiting room for sinners, it was taunting me before annihilating me out of existence.

Still unsure of how to cast a spell that matched my feelings, I faked my confidence and I stood my ground. My dead eye revealed a new spell on coin and the outer edges were moving and glowing emerald. The ankh and ring burned my skin with the intensity of my rage.

The Raven flew into view and perched on my shoulder.

"Caw. Your mother wouldn't have wanted this."

"That thing *killed* my mother."

"Enough, child." The Angel's resonant voice throbbed in my mind and they were in front of me between breaths.

"Your mother's sacrifice freed us from the town. May that be a comfort to you."

The Angel's arms surrounded me as did their ever-changing rainbow hues. And with a gust of wind, we were aloft. I longed to feel comfort, but instead, I only felt the chill of their icy grip on my skin. Fatigue overcame me.

Visions of the little girl, now a bit older, flooded my consciousness once more.

I tried to push back, but was overwhelmed by the emotions pushed upon me. Fear had become anger, and anxiety had grown into indifference.

She closed off the world and shut herself up inside the dark corners of her imagination. Her feelings became my burden to bear. My anger and the darkness of her emotions melded into a torrent of self-loathing and rage that smoldered inside me.

I squirmed within the Angel's ferocious hold as I tried to shake off these visions. The Angel held me fast in their unrelenting vice grip.

I had to force myself to feel the gentle pulse from my grandmother's ankh as it sent a warming comfort throughout my body. Ever so slowly, I focused on my grandmother. The visions faltered and dispelled.

We blasted through The Darkness Within's blockade and I heard it screech in pain. We hurtled away from Purgatory at high velocity.

I looked back to see the deadly darkness collapse upon itself and obliterate the spot where we had been a mere heartbeat before. I closed my eyes in silent prayer to thank my mother.

Our flight was so quick and so sudden that I didn't know how far we had traveled.

Freed from the coiled belly of Hell and the liminal space that was the town of Purgatory, all three of us stood on a desolate single-lane road on an open plain in the cold of the sunless day. Pallid earth stretched to the horizon in every direction. Withered bones of shrubs dotted the hard-scrabble soil.

The barren landscape reflected the emptiness inside me.

A faint whisper of morning peeked out over the eastern horizon in dark aquamarine hues. It was still a long way to sunrise.

"I had that thing right where I wanted it!"

"CAW. You were about to die for real, little one."

"I could feel the power of the magic in my relics flow through me. I could have beaten that thing and you stopped me." I pointed my finger right in the Raven's mangy little face.

"The ankh is not yet at full strength. Don't let your small

taste of its power consume you, little Anna." The Raven's aura cooled to a soothing shade of azure.

The Angel's words throbbed in my head. "That heart scarab ring gracing your finger does not stop the body's demise, child."

I had creeping doubts about the Angel's veracity and their ever-changing hues made it hard for my dead eye to read their true intentions. Each time he touched my skin, I was inundated with images of that girl with the hole in her heart.

"The ring only protects your soul from being cleaved from your body." The Raven clarified before pecking dirt and grime off his feathered form.

I fell to my knees on the parched earth and sighed.

The Raven and the Angel looked as if they didn't know what to do. I made them wait as long as I could tolerate before I said anything.

"Why are you helping me? Half the time I feel like you both want me dead and half the time you swoop in to save me."

"The Magnificent Toth granted your line of spellcasters knowledge and power. Enough to even hold us captive." The Raven's small beady black eyes peered into me.

A deep azure with a fringe of emerald flared up around his bird form for just a moment. Magic was keeping him from saying something. Odd that my dead eye hadn't picked up on it sooner.

"And what, exactly, are you?" I glared daggers at both of them.

"Caw. Companions for a long and dangerous journey." His aura was a perfect azure blue. He was speaking from the heart. If whatever he really was had a heart.

I brushed away the moisture from my good eye as my dead eye showed me the dying vestiges of my mother's aura that encircled my mother's ring.

The dust of the trail swirled around my stagnant body. My anger made me feel invincible for just a moment and I almost died for real.

My memories were faded ghosts.

My soul was bruised.

My heart was broken.

My body was worn out.

But I did find out something true. The Raven and Angel were just as beholden to this journey as me.

"Hurry on, Anna. The Darkness Within will find you again."

"And with it, Emma knows where I am too."

I traveled along the scratch of a desert road with an angel, the bringer of light, on my left and a raven who may not be what he says, on my right. My grandmother spoke true, I was traveling with strange company, indeed.

I admired the ring my mother gave me. The metalwork was full of etched inscriptions and was in the shape of a scarab beetle. Two gemstones were held firm within the shape, one a deep sapphire for the body and an amethyst for the head. The last remnants of my mother's aura were fading away. My anger finally started to subside. My cheek felt moist in the dry desert air.

"Thank you."

The Raven turned to face me. "For what, little one?"

"Saving me from my overconfidence."

"Caw. Vows are meant to be kept, little Anna."

Grandmother told me that before the night was over, I was going to have to choose. Choose what? Between the Angel and the Raven? She pushed me away as she touched my heart for the briefest of moments. I didn't remember much from before, but I knew she would never do anything without a purpose.

My mother said to remember that I once loved her. Who is "her"? Emma? Why would I have loved Emma? She was trying to kill me. She used The Darkness Within to murder my mother right in front of me. The Raven and the Angel wouldn't give me a straight answer, even if I did ask them.

Our unlikely trio walked for an eternity on our weary path. The dull gray of the predawn was not getting noticeably lighter. The landscape didn't yield any notable features to gauge distance.

My sense of time and space was lost to the disorientation of this bleak, gritty sameness.

Was there a destination or just more of this incessant horizon?

Were the mountains in the distance ever getting any closer?

Had we always been on this path?

Would we always be on this path?

Maybe what came before was a dream, and this was my Purgatory—my atonement for sins not yet remembered.

Emma and The Darkness Within could kill me at any moment. And here I was on this lonely road; humbled and humiliated. Who was I to think that I could defeat them?

My dead eye showed me something new on the horizon. It didn't exactly radiate an aura, but it did glow with the static pinpricks of random colors.

We came upon a primitive road marker. There were two rough arrows carved into a used headstone. Each had words underneath. I could actually read this language.

One rough-hewn arrowhead pointed to my left, "Regret." And another pointed to my right, "Sorrow."

Perfect. Even the markers here were obscure.

The Raven perched on the top of the marker.

"One path to home. One to continue this journey."

"The path home is life. Your life. The path forward is death. Possibly yours, little one."

"Fantastic. And I suppose neither of you can tell me which is the right path?"

"Caw. Only *you* will know the answer."

The Raven's aura cooled to azure to reassure me he was telling the truth. The Angel remained silent, but their rainbow-hued aura shifted towards crimson, vermilion, and saffron for a moment. Was that a crack of uncertainty in the perfect being?

I stared long and hard at each path. There were no footprints. No indentations of wheels. No indications of which path was the one to take.

Not with my good eye.

I closed my one good eye and my dead eye revealed the shimmering sparks of a vivid violet aura drifting along the path marked Sorrow. Of course.

"Once you choose your path, there is no turning back, child."

The Angel's voice thrummed inside my skull.

My dead eye never lies. A violet aura was true always and always. I may not like what it showed me. But it never lied. As soon as I had made up my mind, I felt a relaxing of that now-familiar tension within my bones of a gateway opening.

I had only taken a step or two along the path of Sorrow when the ground beneath my feet cracked and split open. I started to run as the earth below my feet fell away.

"Hurry on, Anna!"

The Raven was in flight.

I was pushing off of the last vestiges of the crumbling path, and I was barely keeping up.

The Angel remained as calm as ever, hovering above the calamity below them.

I was losing what little footing I had as the intensity of the erosion increased exponentially.

"Faster is better, little one," The Raven screeched in my direction.

I thought I was doing pretty good despite my terror of the situation at hand.

I tried very hard to not think about how high up I was. I concentrated on each and every single little scrap of rock I thought could hold me long enough to keep moving forward.

Until I missed one small step.

The foothold I had on a vanishing pebble evaporated.

I fell with the debris into the openness of infinity. I reached out, grasping for whatever might hold me.

I must have looked pitiful in my free fall.

My arms were flailing, and a solid scream emanated from my tiny frame. I tensed up as I prepared to fall forever.

The wind took a moment to realize I wasn't moving any longer.

I was staring past my feet into the boundless sky that wasn't getting any closer. I held that image in my mind for just a moment. I looked up to see the Angel floating above me, gripping my outstretched arm in theirs.

They tossed me vigorously onto the only part of the path that remained. I tumbled somewhat gracefully onto what seemed to be solid ground. Thankfully, I knew how to tuck and roll. I dusted myself off and stood up. I dug my boots into the graveled soil, still leery of the veracity of the new patch of earth underneath me.

"You are brave to have chosen to continue our journey, little Anna."

The Raven's aura cooled off for a flicker of a moment. Perhaps a sign of admiration?

"That remains to be seen."

Great. Now I sounded like the Raven and the Angel. This place was starting to get to me. Maybe because nearly everything here seemed to want me dead.

The way we had come was nothing but a vestige of my past. Sorrow was the path of my future while Regret now existed solely in my memory of things not done.

Dawn was lurking in the East. My heart and my soul had been through Hell and back and my journey here wasn't done just yet.

A home that I don't quite remember had been so close. A twinge of doubt lingered in the pit of my stomach for a few moments before moving on toward what might be my death.

HOUR NINE : THE FOREST

We had journeyed far beyond the crossroads, yet the scenery remained unchanged in its persistent desolation. The horizon line hadn't budged an inch in my good eye's view since we escaped Purgatory. I could see nothing but the shimmering haze of dusty grains scouring every square inch of this desolate plain that distorted distance and time.

But my dead eye pierced through the veil of mundane reality, revealing a lush forest. Blurry auras sharpened with each blink of my dead eye. The trees themselves seemed to breathe, their trunks expanding and contracting in a slow, hypnotic rhythm. Trees have auras, but this was something different.

"Caw. Be aware, Anna. Dangerous are the trees in the forest no one sees."

If I had to guess, I would say even the trees here would somehow try to kill me. I hoped I was wrong.

The flatland was a dull, endless gray. This forest that only my dead eye could see was immediate. It was a welcome change to see something other than the monotonous span of infinity.

The harmonizing sparkle of these petrified giants was dazzling. The density of leaves left no room for light to penetrate this secret place.

A rustle upon the wind brought with it murmurs of a voice long gone.

"I see you … *Anna.*"

A male voice died as the air calmed.

"Bloody heck."

I looked around and saw only the Raven, the Angel, and the trees.

A slight breeze kissed my cheek.

"I loved you … *Anna.*"

"Who are you?"

"I was once … *family.*"

Hope stirred within a single beat of my heart.

"Father?"

"That was an … *affectionate* term."

I drifted between the cluster of trees, their branches reaching out like welcoming arms. A carpet of soft moss spread out on the path before me.

The Raven's wings beat frantically behind me as he tried to keep up.

"Anna. Wait."

Fractal patterns of branches sprouted from the earth and intertwined themselves together after each of my steps. The magic of the forest surrounded me in its warm embrace.

The forest was no longer just inside the vaporous haze of my dead eye. It was very real. The dense foliage cut me off from the Raven and the Angel before any of us had realized.

"I must tell you ... a *secret*."

The man's voice haunted me. I had never known my father.

Had I?

I continued my dance with the towering titans. They circled me as I moved between their roots and trunks in an unspoken rhythm.

"This is an unwise course of action, child."

The Angel's voice was so distant inside my head that I could only make out the familiar dull thrum, but no words came of it.

A mournful groan of branches grew and connected with each other. The wooden prison tightened around me with every step I took.

The Raven was squawking, but I could no longer make out his words.

There it was again. That familiar warmth of love. Just like when I met my grandmother and mother. Yes, this had to be my father.

"Where are you?"

The leaves fluttered without any wind.

"Here and there … a little bit of *everywhere*."

Gnarled roots intertwined with the fertile earth and moss below my feet. Dense overgrowth parted for me and showed me the way to a father I had forgotten when I woke up in this place.

I arrived at a clearing. The trees all around me were shimmering with life. Before me was a withered, old oak tree. Blackened by time and ravaged by the elements, this ancient one wore its age poorly.

The trunk was hundreds of feet tall. Massive branches formed a solid canopy over this secluded nook. Embedded within the whorls and crevices of the bark was the face of a man frozen in eternal sorrow.

Half-concealed behind a painted porcelain mask, the visage presented a stark duality. While gnarled bark formed weeping eyes and anguished lines on one side, the mask's smooth perfection maintained an ageless, emotionless facade on the other.

From behind this unyielding veil, a single eye gazed outward. It pulsed with an ethereal, crystalline blue light, as if holding secrets of the forest within its depths.

Carved into the bark just below the mask were the words, "Cordelia + Edmund." My mother and my father. I had condemned their names to the hazy shades of things not remembered. I hated this place.

"Daughter."

I looked up into the mask that formed half a face.

"Father." I said the word out of reflex, but I felt no happiness or relief, only the emptiness of a lost child abandoned to the fate of the world.

"What has happened to you?"

"Never mind ... the *suffering*."

The branches wove together into an impenetrable cocoon around me, and the gentle nudge of their tension pulled me closer to the tree that was my father.

"You must ... *remember*."

Spindly branches splintered from the larger ones and shot forth to latch onto my head. Thousands of coarse ends entwined themselves within my hair to cradle my scalp. The branches were warm and comforting against my head.

Images flashed before my mind's eye. Before one could develop fully, another would replace it. I tried to hold on to as many of the images as I could.

Father was handsome.

He loved Mother with all his heart.

There was a secret.

Something awful.

Mother, broken and lost, escaped her life.

Father, full of resentment, abandoned his duties.

I was alone.

Tears rolled down my cheeks uncontrollably as the overload of memories continued to pierce my past and my present. My legs felt weak as I swayed with the enormity of my emotions. My ankh and ring were getting hot. Their power coursed through my body. My body trembled, overwhelmed by the onslaught of emotions that spanned a lifetime I had forgotten.

"Enough."

The air and ground shook with my outburst. The branches groping my head snapped off at their tips, and what remained recoiled back to their original positions, praising the sky. I steadied myself once more.

"I didn't mean ... *harm*."

"Then what did you mean?"

"A *gift* ... and a *secret*."

"What gift? What secret?"

A soft breeze nudged me. I took a feeble step forward and then another. As I approached, the mask broke free from the confines of the bark.

"The gift of seeing... *truth*."

The mask fell, and I plucked it out of the air with my right hand.

"Dead or alive ... eyes are windows to the *soul.*"

"And the soul is truth." I finished my father's sentence out of habit.

"Grandmother used to tell me that growing up."

Up close, I could see the mask had a slight texture that marred its perfection. A worn leather band was carefully hinged to the temples. Hidden behind the sweeping inky black of a tattoo gleamed the beautiful blue gemstone of an eye. The imperfections made the mask mesmerizing and insidious all at once.

"Your memories ... *returned.*"

The bone porcelain mask was too big for my belt of useful things, so I tucked it into my satchel. I stood face-to-face with my father. The mask had concealed the other half of my father's face hewn into the tree trunk. This newly revealed side was twisted and sinewy. This side of his face was anger.

"Emma ... comes for her *sister.*"

The dark rings that made up my father's eyes started to leak sap. Leaves fell n a mad frenzy. The branches that enveloped our private cove crumbled to dust.

The soldiers made of timber that defended me and my father were bleeding black from their bark.

"Wait. *Sister?* Do you mean *me?*"

The Darkness Within had caught up with me yet again. Trees disintegrated into dark creeping tendrils that groped the forest searching for its prey. Once proud and ancient trees crumbled into dust, their essence devoured by creeping tendrils of pure shadow.

"Farewell ... my *child.*"

I stood in the dead center of the chaos of my father's dying forest as The Darkness Within consumed the trees protecting us.

The sap that drenched the tree that was my father gave birth to millions of scarab beetles. They ripped their way free from the musty liquid and began their task of chewing away the wood.

"No. No. *No.*"

The beetles worked with haste as they devoured the tree that was my father.

I let one small whisper take to the wind. "I love you, Father."

The outer perimeter of branches snapped as dark tendrils thrashed and battled with the fragile bark of my father's forest. My dead eye alerted me, but even then, I could barely roll out of the way in time. A deadly barrage of darkness crashed hard into the forest floor where I had been a few moments before.

Again, my grief was on hold as I fought for my life in my dream of death.

Shadow tendrils shot across the forest, shattering bark. Tensile wood creaked and heaved as it parried and returned blows.

I was caught in the middle, scouring for any place that might be safe for even the briefest of moments.

I stepped wrong and landed hard on the ground face-first. I forced myself to sit up. I saw The Darkness Within approaching fast. I spit some dirt out and tried to stand, but wasn't ready to be on my feet just yet.

I held my breath as dozens of tendrils bore down on me.

Darkness filled my dead eye's field of view, and I braced myself for the inevitable.

Roots exploded upwards from the earth to cradle me on all sides. The Darkness Within hit hard against them and disintegrated most of my protection instantly.

I stood up as best as I could and started to focus.

An aura—no, a burst of brilliant fiery vermillion—burned in my peripheral vision above the tree line. I turned to see the Angel with their glorious rainbow aura, wielding a flaming sword to cut through tendrils and branches with equal ferocity.

The Raven swooped in and landed on my shoulder.

"Hurry on, Anna."

"Where? We're trapped here."

"You must see the trees, not the forest." The Raven's beady little eyes stared expectantly at me.

"No. I can't do that. I *won't* do that."

"CAW! He is *alr*—"

In a flash of white light, the Raven exploded into blood and feathers all over me as his aura was snuffed out.

My scream died in my throat as I tried to move.

I had to force myself not to panic. I was covered in fragments of the Raven and his wine-colored blood.

The Raven had been my one constant on this ever-changing journey since I arrived at the graveyard. And now he was simply gone.

"Drat," I cursed under my breath.

My hands were shaking. My dead eye could only see the Angel's aura now.

I needed to get away from this fight. And there was only one way to do so.

I begrudgingly looked at my father's tree in the midst of being devoured by the beetles. The last of my family had been taken from me again.

My dead eye showed a beautiful azure aura escaping towards the heavens from the center of the battle as the beetles finished their work. Within the stream of light, I saw the pinprick kaleidoscope that was my father's soul remain for a blink of an eye before journeying onward. My shoulders relaxed and my mind was calm as I felt the gateway that was once my father's tree open.

My left side was hot. It felt good for a moment to be warm again. When the warmth started to ooze, I realized I'd been hit and was bleeding. Tendrils from The Darkness Within had ruptured a thick branch the size of my body, splintering wooden shrapnel into my face and arm.

I could feel the sharp tingling of dozens of shards of bark embedded in my face and arm. Some fell out as I dodged another assault from The Darkness Within as it battled with an enormous tree directly over me. I sensed the copper ankh starting to repair the damage done to my body.

The wind moved around me, and I was off of my feet and in the Angel's steel-cold grasp once more.

"Their time has passed, child."

My life-force was being drained. Once more my mind was deluged with fractured images of a little girl with the hole in her heart.

She was grown up now and all that life had thrown at her weighed her down. She was a prisoner of her own thoughts and feelings. Indifferent to the world, uncaring to anyone, even herself.

Grief stared to wrap itself around my body in waves, and I tried to shake off these nightmares.

I had to fight.

My grandmother's ankh was warm against my chest, and I felt calm. The images slowly dissipated as I focused on my grandmother's love and kindness.

The Angel slashed and hacked their way through tendrils and branches with the sword in their left hand. They gained some ground, but just barely. They held me aloft just above the tree tops. But we were still engulfed and overwhelmed by the tendrils and branches.

"The time has come for us to part ways, child."

The Angel tossed me aside as they remained stoic in their defiance above me. I fell in slow motion, and watched as The Darkness Within and the branches shredded the Angel's perfect body into wine-colored blood and fragments that spattered across me and half the forest. Their beautiful aura lingered for a moment before turning black and evaporating into nothingness.

Their flaming sword flickered and burned out before falling from the sky.

I had lost everyone now.

I let myself feel the sadness as I descended to the ground between tendrils and timber fighting over little old me.

The Raven was an enigma until the end. The Angel, despite their indifference, did save my life more than once. They were a balance to the Raven's frantic energy. Between the light and the dark, I made this journey. Because of the light and the dark, I survived this long.

And now both were gone.

The Angel's final act was to toss me through the hollowed-out husk of my father's timbered confinement.

A sickening crack of brittle bones breaking filled my ears as I was cast down through the corpse of my father's broken shell.

HOUR TEN : THE SECRET PASSAGE

A flash of lightning.

Then, darkness.

The sky cries soft tears.

The burnt-out husk of a Queen Anne mansion looms high on a hill.

A girl weeps quietly in the shadows by the front veranda.

She starts to hum a melody as I approach. I can't quite place the tune, but it resonates within me like my own breath.

I place one foot on the stairs, then another. The worn wood groans its displeasure under the pressure of my weight.

The girl turns to me and another flash of lightning reveals her face is my face. She embraces me wholeheartedly.

I can't breathe as she squeezes the life from my body.

I shuddered awake with a loud gasp that echoed in the darkness of a small underground alcove.

At long last, I was told the truth. The girl haunting me in my dreams was my sister, Emma.

How could I have forgotten her?

Why was she trying to kill me with The Darkness Within?

What had happened to her?

To my family?

A soft coil of roots had caught me in a gentle embrace. One last gift from my father. The aroma of wet earth penetrated my nose and mouth. I could taste the dank air as I tried to adjust my good eye to this new place.

My father was dead once more. I lingered in this space he had created for me for as long as I dared. I savored the musky aromas and the feeling of safety and comfort. But I had to keep moving. It would only be a matter of time before The Darkness Within found me again.

I plucked the remaining shards of bark out of my arm and face. The wounds stopped bleeding right away, and my ankh would heal them fully soon enough.

My good eye was all but useless, and I could only see flashes of my surroundings with my dead eye. I felt my way along the cramped space.

My first step sunk down into the muddy ground. The deep treads on my boots offered no traction as I slogged forward slowly and deliberately. Each footfall was a battle. I lifted my foot from the sucking earth only to have to repeat the process with my next step. I had to turn sideways to fit into a slim passage. The walls oozed mud and moisture.

My family was dead.

The Raven was dead.

The Angel was dead.

Now I was alone here.

I was covered in their blood, in this secret passage somewhere within a dream that might be my death.

Perhaps I was the one who is dead and is just dreaming?

Despite their flaws, the Raven, the Angel, and I had been through Hell and back together. That was *something*. And now it was over. The companions I relied on for so much of this journey had forsaken me when I needed them most. And not one of my relics was giving me any notion of what to do next.

I felt stronger now. A power coursing through my body that wasn't there before. At first, it was hardly noticeable, but now it has definitely gotten more intense. My father had restored my memories, and I was still trying to process them.

Flashes would come to me in jumbled bits and pieces that mostly made sense. But there were still gaps. It felt good to finally know more about myself and where I came from.

One thing that stood out was my coin. It was my grandmother's spellcaster coin. Passed down through the generations of my family from the Magnificent Toth himself, who gave our world the gift of magic.

This coin was powerful in the right hands. Only the most skilled spellcasters could use it to its fullest potential.

My family had given me what I needed to continue on my sacred journey. Nothing, not even the goddess herself, was going to stop me.

I inched my way along the claustrophobic space, feeling along the contours of the passage walls in the darkness. My dead eye could make out markings along the wall of the inner chamber that might have been a language long ago. The meaning of whatever message was left behind had been long since forgotten.

I compressed myself into the only way forward. Jagged rocks pressed against both my front and back. I scraped my way through the confines of the ever-narrowing passage.

The muddy ground beneath my feet was getting harder to navigate. Each step was excruciatingly slow until I could no longer move.

I glanced down with my dead eye and saw the truth. The mud was black sludge that was gripping my feet. The Darkness Within surged up from the depths in a viscous tide of malevolence that engulfed my lower body.

I was being dragged down. I gripped the uneven surface and held on tight.

I felt the searing pain of tendrils creeping up my calves as The Darkness Within tried to claim me as its victim. My fingers slipped, and I got pulled further under. My left hand caught hold of another outcropping, but my right arm swung free and got overtaken by The Darkness Within.

I closed my good eye and focused on the spellcaster coin, the copper ankh, and the ring. I felt the warm glow of my family's magic flow through my body. The coin's outer layers revolved to show my dead eye runes of spells to cast. The ankh and ring protected my heart and soul.

My mind burned with the imagery of my family dying. I could do nothing but watch as they died over and over again.

Anger followed sadness, and the grief of my solitude wrapped me in the bitterness of despair.

I let myself feel it all. If I could have screamed, I would have yelled so the entire world would have heard me.

I wept at my helplessness.

My vulnerability was on full display, and I hated it.

I knew these were only memories, my memories, tainted and twisted by the darkness within me.

The images played over and over until I finally became numb to their pain, and my mind wandered to the thought of surviving one more moment.

I felt the warmth of my ring and ankh send comfort and healing through my soul.

My dead eye had located a spell on my coin. I opened my mouth to utter the incantation but found I couldn't say the words. The Darkness Within had censored me. I sputtered as a dark tendril choked the life from my helpless body.

I struggled to move. But I couldn't give up just yet.

I saw the colorful prickle of stars as I began to lose consciousness. My mind started to drift off.

No.

I had to stay awake.

I had to fight.

I tried to say the spell quietly to myself in the hopes it might do some good anyway. The tendrils tightened around my throat and leaked through my closed lips into my mouth.

Helplessness washed over me as the darkness drowned me in its oppressive desires. Just like when I was little.

I should have given up.

But I was strong.

One more time.

Silently, like a prayer inside my mind, I asked for the help I needed.

"Hear me O Horus, Protector from Evil. I am Anna. I am the Akh of the prophecy. I command you to obey. Free me from this vile darkness."

My dead eye flared to life and revealed the colorful glow of auras along both walls. Each aura told its story with layers upon layers of emotions and memories etched into the very stones encased in the walls. I opened my good eye and was met with the gaze of one thousand eyeballs embedded within the rocks. The eyes all stared at me with an intensity almost as overwhelming as the Angel's gaze.

All one thousand such eyes burned the curse of their evil eye deep into The Darkness Within. Its grip faltered and loosened before releasing me entirely.

I choked up some black goo as I lay on the soft, warm mud to catch my breath for a moment before standing up.

The walls parted just enough for me to stand freely on the sloppy mess of earth beneath my feet. All the eyes that lined the walls on either side of the passageway were focused on me.

No, not me. They were staring at my satchel. My dead eye showed my father's mask glowing emerald green. I reached inside and pulled it out. The gemstone of an eye glowed like a beacon against the cavern walls. Each of the anonymous eyes spying on me were the exact same color eye as the mask.

With trembling hands, I raised the mask to my face. I pulled it over my head and let it cover my good eye. The soft lining felt warm against my skin. A fresh surge of power flowed through my body. A profound sense of connection washed over me as if the mask not only enhanced my vision, but expanded my consciousness.

I peered ahead along the passage and my good eye revealed glowing embers in all shades of violet floating in front of me. The colors glowed with an intensity even my dead eye couldn't see. I pulled off the mask and looked again. Neither my good eye nor my dead eye could see them without the mask.

The path was clear, and it was easier going now that the walls had receded enough for me to walk freely. I followed the trail until I was facing a wall of water that made no sound. Not one single drop of water made a noise as it journeyed along its path. I tucked the mask in my satchel and examined my situation.

I perched on a narrow ledge mere inches from a raging crystalline blue waterfall. I watched in awe as the soundless fury cascaded endlessly from the cavernous abyss below into the dome above me.

The luminescent violet trail had led me to the waterfall. From there, I lost sight of my path. There was no other way forward.

If only the Raven or Angel were here. One of them might have provided a clue as to my next move. Or pushed me over the edge. I stepped back from the ledge. I was hypnotized by the synchronized rhythm of the water on its journey.

In my vertigo gaze, I saw only the pulsating throb of millions of liters of water flowing freely. There was no past and no present. Only the current, alive with movement.

I looked behind me to see all those eyeballs glaring expectantly at me. Waiting for me to make my decision.

"Goddess, grant me the strength to end this nightmare."

My voice echoed gently, almost soothingly, around me. I closed my eyes and focused on the spellcaster coin, the copper ankh, and the ring. Nothing happened. Whatever was next, I needed no spell.

I put one foot out in front of me and held my breath as I

stepped off the ledge—out into the open space between it and the waterfall.

I was weightless for a heartbeat before I was engulfed by the torrent of water cascading around me. The waterfall flowed around me but did not soak me. It held me aloft but did not drown me.

And, in a single blink of my good eye, the waterfall gently pushed me upward.

I was so light; I felt as if I were flying. It was exhilarating to feel the same freedom as the birds. Between the drops of water falling upwards, I could make out dark green moss growing along the walls of the cavern. Even here, life continued on.

I let myself smile for the first time in a long time.

I looked toward the small point of light that I was rapidly approaching. I was racing forward to face the end of my dream.

Or, perhaps, my death.

HOUR ELEVEN : THE HOUSE

The time had come to face my fate.

My fractured family.

My forgotten sister.

A life I wasn't sure I could even get back to.

The water pounded my body and pushed me up until I surfaced inside a decorative fountain.

The goddess had cleansed my soul. My sins had been absolved, and my hatred and anger scrubbed from the shadows of my mind. I was whole again. I sat in the knee-high water, thanking the goddess for her blessings.

I stepped down from the fountain onto a white and black checkerboard marble floor. I was inside a house. Not just any house. This was the Queen Anne from my dream. Instead of a broken, worn-down husk of a home, this one was in its full glory.

Above me, electric lights hummed from within the ornate chandelier as they contentedly illuminated the room. Rich tapestries adorned the walls, their threads weaving tales of our family's lore. Vibrant oil paintings by long-dead masters filled in the faces of generations past along the hallowed halls.

I was *home.*

A joyful tear tried to creep out of my eyes, but I held onto it for now.

I noticed a painting of my grandmother in a cozy alcove tucked off to the side of the main entrance. I approached the gilded frame and reflected in a moment of silence. The artist captured the warmth of my grandmother's suffused saffron aura in an impressionist style.

A massive white marble fireplace dominated the room. Carved into its face was the history of the gods and goddesses who guided our bloodline of spellcasters. Above it hung a painting of my mother, father, and me. The style was more modern. The brush strokes were calmer and more dignified. My family was all in black. Mother, demure as ever, held a small daruma doll with one eye missing on her lap. I stood off to her right, holding her hand and doing my best to look up. Father towered over us in a protective posture. His hair was unkempt and the sadness in his eyes lingered with me long after I left the painting.

As I moved further into the house, my copper ankh glowed and filled me with strength. My heart scarab ring tingled with its power on my finger. My spellcaster coin tucked into my belt of useful things glowed emerald green in my dead eye's view, ready to find the right spell. Now that I had my memories and power back, by merely glancing at my spell-caster coin with my dead eye's magical vision, I could see the spells and cast them instantaneously.

I paused at the bottom of the grandiose staircase and looked up to see the twin trees from the graveyard immortalized in stained glass. The vibrant tree glowed with life and the barren tree, even with the light coming from behind, was dull and lifeless. The sinews of the fiber of their beings were twisted together so that one couldn't exist without the other. Small trickles of water streamed from the bark of the vibrant tree while blood oozed from the bark of the barren tree. The land beneath the vibrant tree was lush and green. The land that touched the barren tree was a dusty patch of earth.

"Our family's secret, emblazoned in shards of glass for all to see. How *ironic*."

The voice was so close in tone to my own as it reverberated throughout the house. It took me a moment to realize it was not me thinking or saying these words. It was *her*.

"Hello, Emma."

Striding down the soft, blood-red velvet steps was Emma. She was clad in a long, flowing black dress that appeared to devour light. A sharp, onyx-feathered headpiece that scraped the sky crowned her head.

As I stood there, staring at the embodiment of darkness before me, my eyes were drawn to the wings sprouting from Emma's back. They were a twisted mockery of an angel's wings, jagged shards of obsidian cutting into the air around her. They seemed to absorb the shadows around them, pulsating with an unsettling energy that made my skin crawl.

"Hello, *sister.*" Emma's grating voice pierced my ears so sharply that I instinctively checked to see if they were bleeding.

At the base of her throat, a silver ouroboros necklace gleamed in the soft incandescent lighting. She did not have an aura. No glimmer, no wisp, not a sparkle or hint of any color surrounding my sister.

"What is this place?"

Emma looked older than me by a good decade. The lines of maturity had started to crack the contours of her otherwise smooth face.

"My dying wish."

She smiled to herself proudly.

"You tormented our family. You killed the Raven and the Angel."

She stopped dead on the landing and sneered into my soul.

"*You* actually miss those specters of good and evil sitting on your shoulder?"

Emma took another few steps down towards me. Her viscous black dress hugged the stairs, which made her appear to float.

"You will pay for what you did to *me*, Anna."

Her dark crystalline amethyst eyes burned with her hatred. Emma's black dress and crown began pulsating. With a sound like tearing silk, inky tendrils erupted from Emma's dress toward me. I rolled to one side and stood up in a ready stance.

The tendrils lashed out with terrifying speed. A second onslaught destroyed the husk of an armored warrior behind me.

My dead eye showed me the violent blood crimson of The Darkness Within only after it extended past Emma's body. But Emma herself remained illusive to my dead eye's view.

As Emma's assault intensified, I felt a surge of warmth emanating from my ankh. It pulsed against my skin in time with my racing heartbeat, a beacon of hope amidst the encroaching darkness.

My dead eye revealed runes along the rim of my spellcaster coin in the emerald green glow of magic. Words rose unbidden to my lips, ancient and powerful, the language of Toth himself. The power of my family that had come before flowed through my body and gave me fortitude.

I balled up as I braced for impact but all the tendrils disintegrated before they could touch me.

The Darkness Within shrieked in agony.

I stood up, feeling a bit more confident. I was no longer defenseless against this evil being. And I didn't need to utter spells out loud any longer.

"One defense spell does not make you our grandmother, Anna."

Another assault of tendrils, all of which shot around and past me. My dead eye saw them turn back towards me. I spun around, and the spellcaster coin lit up a defensive spell once more. The tendrils splattered harmlessly onto the floor.

I turned back to my sister. If she was concerned, she was not letting me see it. What I did see with my dead eye, though, was that her once-high crown was much shorter now. Was I slowly chipping away at The Darkness Within?

"You are so *weak,* Anna. I captured a god and his fallen morning star and subjugated them to do my bidding. What makes you think that little Anna can prevail over *me?*"

Emma let out a cackle. I went to take a step toward her and was pulled off my feet. My satchel fell off my shoulder and landed hard on the cold stone of the floor.

I looked down to see that one of the black tiles had reached out and grabbed my leg. It must have gotten under my defensive spell.

And now it wasn't letting go. My dead eye showed my sister was pulsating with another attack. And while I couldn't see her aura, I could sense this was going to be the biggest assault so far.

The Darkness Within was pulling me down into the floor. Both of my legs were bound and it wouldn't be long before my hands and arms would be fettered. The poison of my tainted past rained down upon my mind.

But it was too late. The Darkness Within had already forced me to face my dark days and it could no longer harm me.

The phantoms-of-the-mind attack dissolved before they could materialize. My head pounded with a dull throbbing that I pushed back as much as I could.

I was still ensnared by The Darkness Within, and I was running out of options. A gleam of blue caught my eye. The mask my father had given me had fallen free from my satchel.

I lunged for the mask, but it was just out of reach. So close. I tried again, using as much leverage as I could muster.

I snatched the mask just before another black tile could absorb it. I pulled it over my good eye.

The world lit up in my good eye. Everything I could see with my dead eye was amplified. The darkness of night burned away, and I could see out of both eyes as if it were daylight.

My fatigue from struggling with the tendrils was gone. I felt more alive than I ever had. All my senses were at their peak.

I gazed down at the tendrils that bound me to the tile, and I was released instantly. I heard The Darkness Within scream in agony.

"How is this possible? How did you get the Mask of Horus?!"

With my newfound clarity of vision, I set my eyes upon Emma.

"Bloody heck."

The thing standing on the stairs was not my sister. It was a chaotic ocean of evil. The Darkness Within was nothing but a cauldron of lies, deception, and self-loathing pretending to be my Emma.

"You do not deserve such power, Anna."

Emma's body convulsed and distorted as the Nightmare Raven burst forth from the inky depths of her onyx crown. The Nightmare Raven's mangy white feathers dripped with viscous black ooze. It let out a piercing shriek as it took flight, circling above us with a malevolent intent.

As the Raven ascended, the wings on Emma's back cracked and peeled away from her body like a second skin. The dark wings that had once sprouted from Emma's back now unfurled from the Nightmare Angel's shoulders, stretching out to their full, terrifying span. With a flick of its wrist, an obsidian sword solidified in the Nightmare Angel's hand, drawn forth from the very depths of its menacing form.

The two nightmarish entities now stood before me, separate from Emma, but no less terrifying. The Nightmare Raven continued to circle overhead, its beady eyes fixated on me with a hunger that sent shivers down my spine. The Nightmare Angel, with its wings of darkness and sword of obsidian, regarded me with a cold, calculating gaze. I felt the power radiating off of them, a tangible force that seemed to suck the very light from the room.

A terror reignited from within my bones and I had to restrain my urge to run at the very sight of the twisted monstrosities.

Why the bloody heck was I still scared of these ghastly shades from a nightmare within this dream?

The Nightmare Raven swooped toward me and yanked my father's mask from my face with its deft claws. I reached out to snatch it back but couldn't match its speed. The protection of the artifact was ripped away, leaving me exposed and vulnerable. My vision crashed back to normal, and I was blinded in both eyes.

My reflexes were much slower without the mask on. I still couldn't open my good eye, and my dead eye was a bit sluggish. My spellcaster coin lit up a spell targeting the Nightmare Raven and sent it flying through an antique vase. I heard my father's mask clatter to the floor amongst the shards of pottery.

My dead eye tingled back to life only to reveal the Nightmare Angel standing before me. I turned to face it only to be met with the crisp edge of his blade piercing my heart.

"Drat."

There was a moment of surreal stillness before pain exploded through my chest. I wheezed for breath as its soulless eyes bored into me, and it thrust the weapon all the way through my body and out the other side.

I slumped to the floor. Agony burned within my entire body. Even my copper ankh was overpowered by such a blow.

My spellcaster circled to different spells, but I just couldn't focus. The Nightmare Raven had recovered and was pecking and tearing at my flesh as my lifeblood drained away.

The Darkness Within towered over me.

"Foolish child. This is *my* dream."

The Darkness Within unleashed another barrage of razor-sharp tendrils that penetrated my fragile and exposed body.

I was painting the floor red with each pump of my heart.

As I lay there, my life ebbing away, I felt my relics struggling against the inevitable.

The ankh was lukewarm against my skin in a futile attempt to knit flesh and seal my wounds. But it was not enough.

My heart scarab ring was straining to hold my heart and soul together. It burned on my finger with desperate intensity, trying to tether my fleeing soul to my failing body.

My spellcaster was showing me all the ways I could react. Runes flashed by in a dizzying array of potential spells and countermeasures. But it was like watching a book flip by too fast to read, each possibility slipping away before I could grasp it.

This time, I had no more energy.

This time, I really was dead.

HOUR TWELVE : THE VERANDA

My heart had ceased beating in time with my rhythm.

My brain was soothing me with freshly recovered memories gifted to me by my father.

Peace descended upon my being.

I had expected darkness but saw only warm light everywhere.

I saw Grandmother so clearly.

Her eyes shone so brightly.

Her smile radiated around her.

"My dearest, Anna. I love you and I will see you soon enough."

She gave me a kiss on my forehead. And hugged me tightly.

"But it's not yet your time."

The warmth of her love flowed through the copper ankh and into my corpse.

My heartbeat returned with an almost deafening resonance.

My dead eye opened and revealed to me once more its kaleidoscope vision of auras and hidden truths.

The gaping wound that had been my demise began to knit itself closed, flesh and sinew weaving together in an intricate dance of regeneration.

Air rushed into my lungs, sweet and sharp. Each breath felt like a renewal with potential and vibrant energy.

I intuitively reached out for my father's mask.

Time had slowed for the world, but not for me. The Darkness Within and its minions moved in slow motion to react to my resurrection.

I slid my father's gift, the Mask of Horus, over my good eye. The world lit up once more into a vivid, lucid dream for me. The darkness was no longer a threat to me.

I peered into their eyes and only saw the abyss of wickedness churning inside each one of them. The rage within them was a living thing, writhing and gnashing, threatening to consume everything in its path. Tendrils of darkness reached out, trying to ensnare my mind and soul.

I wouldn't allow it to take hold of me ever again.

I set the gaze of truth upon The Darkness Within. Pure and unassailable, it radiated from the Mask of Horus in waves of golden light. The Darkness Within withered before the fury of my judgment.

My ears registered a pitch so high it was almost out of my range of hearing. I realized The Darkness Within and his nightmares were screaming as they were all vaporized out of existence.

I closed my eyes. A small tear leaked out from my good eye. I carefully removed the mask. The world went back to the dim light of night.

"Thank you." I kissed the mask gently and pretended it was my father.

As time resumed its normal cadence for me, I felt my body relax and the release of tension of one more gateway opening.

Was my dead sister just a figment of my desire in this dream?

I sat in the pool of my blood while my body continued to stitch itself back together, and my senses returned to normal.

"Thank you, Grandmother."

The tears flowed freely now. I let go of my sadness and anger in a deluge of salty water that streamed from my good eye.

As my crying subsided, I realized it had an echo. No, not an echo. Someone else was here. And they were crying too.

But where? This was a huge mansion of a house. How could I find them in my condition?

My dream. The girl from my dream was on the veranda crying. Maybe it's Emma.

I clung to the railing as I navigated down the stairs. I hobbled through the elaborate entry towards the front doors.

"Emma!"

I pulled the hand-carved wood and leaden-glass door back with a strain I worried would rip my chest open again. The heavy wood creaked and groaned, as if reluctant to reveal its secrets.

I was on a porch that matched every detail of my dream. Weathered planks that seemed to whisper tales of bygone days. Intricate latticework that cast web-like shadows. In the distance, the soft pastels of dawn painted the horizon.

Strange that I couldn't see her aura with my dead eye.

I gravitated to where I thought I heard the sound coming from. With unsteady feet, I meandered across the timeworn wooden floorboards. Exhausted and wary of a trap, I slowly crept around the corner.

There she was: on the side veranda. Her form appeared both solid and ephemeral, as if she might dissolve into mist at any moment. Quiet sobs wracked her body, each one a mournful melody that reverberated within my soul.

"Emma. It's Anna. I'm finally here." My voice was barely above a scratchy whisper, yet seemed to echo across the vastness of our disparate journeys.

I looked at my sister for the first time. She was a reflection of me. Beautiful with her dark hair and pale skin. I could only see one of her lavender-colored eyes as her hair hid the left side of her face. At the base of her throat was an ouroboros necklace that seemed oversized for her small frame.

I put my arms around my sister and embraced her with all my love. She sniffled a bit before returning my hug.

She looked so tiny and fragile. I tried not to hold her too tightly.

"I am so glad you found me, sister."

It felt so good to finally feel my sister's embrace.

"Me too, Emma. I *love* you more than anything in the world."

Her grip around me tightened, and I reciprocated.

I realized I had waited my entire life for this moment.

"Oh, Anna."

I noticed Emma was squeezing me too hard.

"I *hate* you more than anything in the world."

Emma's embrace, once a longed-for comfort, now became a vice of inhuman strength, crushing my breath from my lungs. Panic welled up in the pit of my stomach.

"I-I can't breathe."

"That is the idea, *sister.*"

My face met hers. She glared at me with a twisted smile. Her hair had been thrown back and I could see all of her face now. She was missing her left eye, the one opposite mine. Where her aura should have been was a hole in my dead eye's vision.

"Father did not tell you, did he? I am your *twin*, Anna. You killed me before I was born."

Fek. No wonder she didn't have an aura. She was never born. She never had the spark of life to ignite her aura. Emma, my beautiful twin, was a what-if, a dream of a person that never came to be. And yet, impossibly and terrifyingly, here she stood as real as me and filled with a hatred born from an existence unlived.

"This place is my dying wish. I made it as I gasped my last breath in our mother's womb."

My wounds started to reopen, and my ribs strained under the pressure of her embrace.

"I ripped your eye from your skull. I needed to see the outside world since you condemned me to be a Void Soul."

"No, that can't be *true!*"

One of my ribs cracked as the shock of her words reverberated through my body.

"But it is, my dear little Anna." A wicked smile pierced the lower half of her face.

"M-my dead eye. Y-you gave me the gift of my dead eye, Emma." Blood trickled down the edge of my mouth. What little energy I had left was leaving me, and I had no choice but to slump into my sister's death grip on my body.

"Now it is my turn to live out there while you perish in this fading ember of my last dream."

My long-dead twin sister. Even though she was trying to kill me, I still felt nothing but love for her.

I coughed up blood, and Emma continued to crush my body. She hated me with all her soul, yet I loved her with all of mine.

I closed my eyes and moved my face closer to hers. In that moment, suspended between heartbeats, a lifetime of emotions washed over me. I crossed the chasm of time and fate that separated us to kiss her gently on the lips.

"I love you, Em."

Emma released her death grip on me and stepped back. I staggered backward but was able to remain standing on wobbly legs.

"*You* do not get to call me that. *You* murdered me. *You* abandoned me! I *hate* you, Anna."

Her words pierced me deeper than the sword that killed me. Anger tried to rise up inside of me but was quelled by my overwhelming sense of compassion for my sister, whom I loved so very much.

"I didn't kill you, Emma. You died." Streams of tears flowed freely from my good eye.

"You lie."

"Mother and Father loved you so much. Their hearts broke when you died."

"It is too late, Anna. My dream is nearly at an end. The last breath of my dream evaporates into eternity at the dawn."

I reached out to Emma, but she batted away my hand.

"It is *my* time to live! I will conquer the world with the Emerald Tablet in my hands. You will *not* win, Anna."

"I'm not here to win. Grandmother sent me here to *save* you, Emma. She stands guard over my body out there until I return."

"You lie, Anna. Grandmother cast every spell she could think of to keep me dead and my memory nothing but dew drops on the morning grass. I will make them all pay for what happened to me."

"Emma, she was trying to help you. I'm trying to help you. My memories are still a bit fractured, but I do know Grandmother used her wisdom and skills to try and save you."

"Mother and Father could not have cared less after I died. They had *you*. I saw it here with my dead eye."

"What you didn't see was our mother was too broken-hearted to even care for herself after you died."

"Another lie." Emma's eye widened as she stepped back from me.

"Father abandoned me and locked himself up inside the prison he made for himself inside his mind."

"No." Emma was trembling.

"Emma, you gave me one of my greatest gifts, my dead eye. It has saved me more times than I can count."

"More lies, Anna."

"Grandmother restored my soul. Mother restored my heart. Father restored my memories. But I still have a hole in my life without you by my side."

Emma knelt down on the coarse grain of the wooden veranda.

"You lie, Anna," Emma whispered so quietly my ears barely heard the words.

"What does *your* dead eye tell you, Emma?"

Emma's head slumped down as the weight of truth bore down on her twisted version of events.

"I didn't remember how much I missed you until I was standing here with you again, Emma. I've been living my life for both of us."

"It is too late to save me. I am already dead."

She stared up at me with uncertainty building behind her solitary eye.

"Our family sacrificed everything so I could be here. I passed through the midnight of my soul on my journey to save *you*, Emma."

"When Father restored your memories, why did he leave out the fact that we are twins?" A tear leaked down the side of her face from her good eye.

Why had Father kept that memory from me? Even his gift of restoring my memories was woven with mysteries to unravel.

"I don't know. Ours is a family of spellcasters and secrets. All I am certain of is that I do love you, Emma. I've had a hole in my heart my entire life, a sadness I could never quite place, an aloneness that could never be filled by anyone but you."

She knelt there by herself, trembling in the cold of the morning light. How I wished we could have lived a life together. The grief of a life not lived leaked from my good eye.

"We all love *you* so very much. *I* love you more than anything else in the world."

I said a silent prayer of forgiveness to the goddess.

An echo of my grandmother whispered to me. "Gazing upon a Void Soul with dead eyes reverses the curse of eternal damnation."

I inched the Mask of Horus out of my satchel as I held my attention firmly on my sister. She held her hands to her face, and I slipped the mask over my dead eye.

The world fell into the sleep of eventide as my dead eye showed me all my sister's demons suffocating her.

I wept as I cast the gaze of Horus upon Emma.

Emma's Void Soul shattered as I emancipated her soul from annihilation. The spark of her saffron and violet aura illuminated the world in a brilliant burst of light and energy for the very first time.

EPILOGUE : THE DAWN

Birds sang to me as I awoke from the prison of my dream. Pastel hues of the sunrise outside the window glowed with the fresh optimism of the new day. I inhaled deeply and savored the feeling of my first breaths in this body. A real body.

Soft cloth caressed my skin. My warm flesh pulsated with the vibrations of life. I did a lazy stretch and yawned. This body was a perfect fit. I thought it might be more awkward, but it all felt so natural. As if I had lived my whole life in this body.

Grandmother's copper ankh was a comfort around my neck. It was stitching up the physical vestiges of battle. The mental and emotional anguish would take longer to heal.

Mother's heart scarab ring felt natural on my finger. It beat in time with my heart and provided me a measure of soothing comfort I did not think was possible.

The spellcaster coin was tucked safely in the belt of useful things. Its soft emerald glow in the corner of my dead eye's vision reminded me it was ready for anything.

I sat up slowly and took in the room.

My room.

Dust drifted along the sunbeams that warmed me against the chill of the winter's morn. My body was a few years older than in the dream. The room was lived in with a few clothes and life's debris scattered in all the right places.

There was a small library with grimoires and books on art, science, and philosophy fighting for space on dusty shelves.

An old-fashioned desk was tucked in a corner with work spread out on it, ready for me to reprise the work begun.

Talismans and relics were scattered in nooks and crannies. I saw sparks of all the colors of the rainbow within those crystals and metals crafted as protectors and aides to spellcasters. Ossuaries reverently displayed our ancestors in their spaces next to the bookcase.

An elderly woman sat quietly in a rocking chair at the foot of the bed. She had been dead for some hours now.

Grandmother sacrificed her life to save me. She was a wise and powerful spellcaster, but even this spell was too much for her venerable body. I pulled her shawl from the back of the chair over her shoulders and closed her watchful eyes for the last time.

"Thank you, Grandmother."

Grandmother's soul was elsewhere. She was all around me now, woven into the fabric of the universe once more.

I put my hand on her shoulder and kissed her on her forehead. Her body returned to dust now that her commitment to the sacred task had been fulfilled. The ouroboros amulet that had been around her neck gleamed from within her ashes. I picked it up and dusted it off. It flashed a silver smile at me. I slid the leathery cord around my neck and let it fall to my chest. It encircled the copper ankh perfectly as both glowed green for a moment in my dead eye's vision.

I sauntered over to the little desk and picked up the Emerald Tablet. A gift from the Magnificent Toth himself. It was the source of all magic that had been handed down to the generations of spellcasters in our family before me.

The stone was warm to the touch, pulsating with energy. It was beckoning me to bring forth the magic hidden within the familiar runes. I allowed a smile to creep onto my face as I dreamed of what was to come.

In the shadows of another corner was a full-length mirror with a gilded gold frame. Hand-carved angels warned of the dangers within, while demons taunted anyone foolish enough to turn away. The mirror was shattered, its glass shards strewn carelessly on the wooden floor. The Mirror of Forgotten Dreams was a one-way trip. Now this ruined relic was useless, the spell broken forevermore.

I looked out the second-story window and surveyed the forest of snow-covered trees protecting the house. The sun peeked over the frozen tops of the jagged cluster of petrified soldiers waiting patiently until the next time they were called to duty. Soft clouds wafted up into the heavens as the frost burned up in the morning light.

Last night was the longest night of the year. The only time Grandmother could have cast the correct spell with the right relics.

The Raven and the Angel kept their vows despite being conscripted against their will. Loyal until the very end. Without them, I would never have been reunited with my sister.

My family had sacrificed everything for me. To save me.

I had been resurrected with a renewed sense of purpose.

Mother and Father were still out there, somewhere, and I would find them.

My sins had been absolved.

I was energized to be *alive*.

A tempest was burning in the pit of my soul.

Today was a new dawn.

A fresh start.

And I was ready to conquer the world.

AURA COLORS & MEANINGS

Aura colors can be highly personal in their meaning and may vary from person to person. The following is true for most interpretations:

CRIMSON (RED): Anger, rage, barren, power. *Also:* life, energy, victory.

VERMILION (ORANGE): Fear, anxiety, warning.

SAFFRON (YELLOW): Joy, excitement, confidence.

Emerald (Green): Life, magic, renewal, fertility, regeneration, vegetation.

Azure (Blue): Truth, loyalty, serenity.

Violet (Purple): Sky, cosmos, infinity, intuition, one with the universe.

Black: Death, underworld, night.

White: Holiness, purity, omnipotence, sacred.

Rainbow: Deception, lies, secrets. *Also:* all encompassing.

Aura colors sometimes intermingle with more than one color for more complex emotions.

ABOUT NICHOLAS J. NAWROTH

Drawing from his lifelong fascination with mythology and dreams, Nicholas J. Nawroth weaves a mesmerizing tale that explores the shadows of the human psyche and the otherworldly beings that dwell within. His visual story-telling skills, honed since childhood, breathe life into the ethereal creatures and haunting landscapes that populate his dark fantasy world.

When he's not crafting stories or art, Nick enjoys spending time with his wife and their beloved doggies, who inspired his children's picture book series, The Everyday Adventures of Papa & Paws®.

Readers can find more of his work on his website at NicholasJNawroth.com.

ACKNOWLEDGMENTS

This book was a lot of hard work and late nights. It would have never become a "real" book without the following kind folks who helped along the way: my beautiful bride, Ellen, Xander Hildenbrandt, Sabrina Wichner, Amy Reeves, Michael Murray, and Dale L. Roberts.

Thank you all so much for your support and encouragement on this long and winding journey.